Sun Father
Corn Mother

Sun Father Corn Mother

A Novel

Kirk Reeve

Sunstone Press

SANTA FE

Sunstone books may be purchased for educational, business, or sales promotional use.
For information please write: Special Markets Department, Sunstone Press,
P.O. Box 2321, Santa Fe, New Mexico 87504-2321.

Book and cover design › Vicki Ahl
Body typeface › Sylvan
Printed on acid-free paper
∞
eBook 978-1-61139-431-3

Library of Congress Cataloging-in-Publication Data

Names: Reeve, Kirk, 1934- author.
Title: Sun Father, Corn Mother : a novel / by Kirk Reeve.
Description: Santa Fe : Sunstone Press, [2015] | Summary: "Fourteen-year old
    Running Antelope encounters harsh treatment by conquistadors during his
    experiences as a Hopi guide for the Spanish expedition that "discovers"
    the Grand Canyon"-- Provided by publisher.
Identifiers: LCCN 2015032262 | ISBN 9781632930910 (softcover : alk. paper)
Subjects: | CYAC: Hopi Indians--Fiction. | West (U.S.)--Discovery and
    exploration--Spanish--Fiction.
Classification: LCC PZ7.R25575 Su 2015 | DDC [Fic]--dc23
LC record available at http://lccn.loc.gov/2015032262

Sunstone Press is committed to minimizing our environmental impact on the planet. The paper used in this book is from responsibly
managed forests. Our printer has received Chain of Custody (CoC) certification from: The Forest Stewardship Council™ (FSC®),
Programme for the Endorsement of Forest Certification™ (PEFC™), and The Sustainable Forestry Initiative® (SFI®).

The FSC® Council is a non-profit organization, promoting the environmentally appropriate, socially beneficial and economically viable
management of the world's forests. FSC® certification is recognized internationally as a rigorous environmental and social standard for
responsible forest management.

WWW.SUNSTONEPRESS.COM
SUNSTONE PRESS / POST OFFICE BOX 2321 / SANTA FE, NM 87504-2321 /USA
(505) 988-4418 / ORDERS ONLY (800) 243-5644 / FAX (505) 988-1025

For the Little People of Peace

Prologue

The Little People of Peace wait quietly in the darkness, crowded together on the mesa's edge. Men and women pray in muffled tones, their arms extended toward the east. Shivering children sigh with relief at the first sparkle of light as grandmothers lift babies high into the air.

The blackness of night slowly gives way to gray dawn. As bright rays turn the sandstone mesa a yellowish pink, Running Antelope stretches out his arms and gazes at the coming of day. "Oh, Sun Father!" His voice is between that of a boy and a man. "I thank Great Power for making you. It is good what you do for my people. You warm us. We see by your light. You help our corn grow. I am happy to greet you."

From the corner of his eye he sees the basket tray his mother holds out to him. He reaches into it and takes out a handful of cornmeal, pausing to again look at the sunrise before throwing the coarse powder into the still air. Others of the mesa-top village also empty their hands of cornmeal and watch the offering drift in clouds down the vertical side until it disappears from view. Sun Father has put on the skin of the yellow fox and is emerging from his eastern kiva to begin another sacred journey across the sky.

LATE JULY
1540

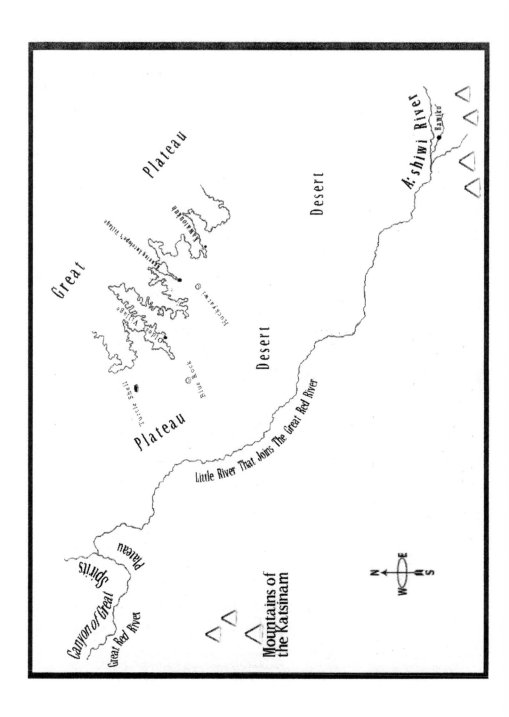

1

Running Antelope felt Father's firm hand on his shoulder. "We must go," he was told in a hushed tone. He followed his parents and Mother's younger brother along the sandy pathway between kivas and houses. Sister's husband, and Sister who was holding their baby, were close behind him. Their home was at the mesa's south end, the last of a long row of dwellings made of fist-size stones. It consisted of two rooms in a two-story terrace style. The larger room, used for eating and sleeping, was at ground level. The smaller room and its porch were on top, and were for food preparation and storage.

As Mother and Sister climbed the outside ladder to prepare the morning meal, Father pushed aside the rabbitskin blanket hanging in the larger room's doorway and stepped inside. Running Antelope waited for his uncle Two Horns Lowered and his sister's husband Rain Walk to enter before joining them. The four sat down cross-legged on the smooth clay floor facing each other. Father spoke first. "It is a short walk to Kawaioukuh. We will arrive when Sun Father is looking down on our heads. Our friends will welcome us and invite us to stay the night. The day that follows will see us on our way to Hawikú."

Two Horns Lowered cleared his throat before he spoke. "The long walk to Hawikú is dangerous for so few of us. The loads we carry will give Old Enemies much reason to attack."

Father nodded, a sober expression on his sun-darkened face. "We will be watchful and ready to fight, and we will ask our Kawaioukuh brothers to accompany us. They trade with the A:shiwi just as we do." Running Antelope listened with the understanding that leaving the safety of their village was dangerous. He had journeyed many times with his father to hunt or trade. For each long walk, Father demanded that he be watchful for Old Enemies—bands of nomads who steal and kill.

Father turned to face Rain Walk. "You will stay here. Our corn needs you, and so does my daughter. We will return before our snake brothers are asked to make our prayers known to the Cloud People."

Mother and Sister entered the room with a warm bowl of cornmeal mush and a basket tray of blue corn piki bread. While everyone ate, Mother spread a cotton blanket on the floor and filled its center with food for the journey. There were cornhusks filled with cooked cornmeal, thin sheets of crisp, sweet piki rolled in pairs, and small sacks of cornmeal for use in mush and stews. With its four corners tied together with yucca cord, the blanket became a food sack to be carried over a shoulder. When the meal was finished, Father nodded at the sack. "You will carry this," he said to Running Antelope. "Two Horns Lowered and I will carry the jars and bowls."

Running Antelope knew that the sacks of pottery were heavy. The jars and bowls were wrapped in cornhusks, and there were many of them. A sack of pottery would soon feel like a sack of stones. "My father, I can help carry the jars and bowls," he volunteered anyway.

Father smiled, "We will each have much to carry."

Running Antelope followed the others outside carrying the food sack over his right shoulder. His water gourd, bow, and quiver of arrows hung by deerskin straps behind his left shoulder. His left hand gripped a slightly curved and smoothly carved piece of cottonwood as long as a man's arm and as thick as a man's wrist. It could be used as a club for fighting, or as a throwing stick for hunting rabbits and other small game. He wore only a breechcloth and a headband, both of coarse, cotton cloth. Father and Two Horns Lowered were similarly equipped and dressed.

At fourteen summers, Running Antelope was almost the height of his father and uncle, who were not tall. Like the two men, he was thin at the waist and muscular in the arms and shoulders. Also, as with the men, his black hair was long and tied in a knot at the back of the neck. His handsome brown face radiated excitement, and he grinned broadly as he walked with Mother and Rain Walk past friends and neighbors to the mesa's edge. There began the steep footpath down the vertical side.

A small crowd of villagers greeted them, including Running Antelope's grandfather and older uncle. Arriving at the same time were two men also equipped for traveling, both of the Snake Clan, like Father. Big Bull Snake was heavy-set and wide-of-shoulder, and carried a stout walking stick. He had been Father's friend since childhood and greeted everyone with warmth in his voice and a smile spread over his wide face. "My good friends!" he thundered. "You are ready, and so are we!"

His younger brother Two Snakes, a brawny, long-legged man six summers older than Running Antelope, smiled and nodded his greeting. He carried a rabbit stick as well as bow and quiver. Both men carried sacks of pottery.

With the shouts of well-wishers sending them on their way, the five travelers started down the twisting stone steps of the narrow footpath with Father in the lead. After several sharp turns, the well-worn stepping-stones paralleled the mesa wall at a steep angle. The five moved slowly and carefully, balancing each downward step with the loads on their backs. Beginning about halfway down, the path reversed itself several times and the angles of descent were less, enabling them to move a little faster. Sure-footed, they gradually increased their speed to a fast walk as the path emptied onto the desert floor.

Moving away from the rocky base of the mesa, they walked by clusters of squash and melons spread across the sandy soil in the path of underground water flows that reached the surface as a spring a short distance beyond. Upon arriving at the spring, Running Antelope filled his gourd, took a long drink, refilled it, and sealed its small opening with a corncob. He then scooped up water in both hands and threw it toward the village as he whispered, "Cloud People...thank you for bringing rain to our corn." The others did the same. Then, in single file, they continued on in the direction of the morning sun.

On both sides of them were small patches of corn and cotton. The plants were still young and close to the ground, their roots reaching deep into the soil in search of moisture. The travelers waved at friends and neighbors already working to loosen the uppermost topsoil around the plants, or checking for fresh mounds left by field rats and gophers. Running Antelope spotted his mother's corn patch that he had helped plant. "My father!" he called out, breaking the silence they had maintained since leaving the spring. "I asked my friends to keep the rats and crows away from our corn while we are gone!" Father nodded and grunted his approval.

Leaving the green patches behind, they angled off to the right to a well-worn path heading southeast. The vast, arid land appeared to be flat when looking down from their village. When walking the land, however, there were ridges and mounds to climb or go around, and dry streambeds and deep ravines to cross. The sandy soil was thinly covered with ankle-high desert grass. Shrubs, cacti, and yucca plants grew independently or in clusters.

Sun Father was two hands above the horizon when Father announced, "There is Huckyatwi!" He nodded to his right at a tall butte rising abruptly above the surrounding land. "Brother Badger is guiding us!"

Running Antelope glanced at the butte every few steps, looking for the angle of vision that would enable him to see the form of a badger in its shape. "Yes!" he soon exclaimed. "There is the badger!"

ਮ ਮ ਮ

Running Antelope shaded his eyes with his forearm to confirm that the summer sun was directly overhead before gazing again along the rocky base of the huge mesa they had reached. "I see corn and cotton!"

"Ayih!" Big Bull Snake cheered from a few paces in front of him. "Our little walk is about to end! My feet and back are happy!"

Kawaioukuh's mesa was much wider than the narrow mesa of Running Antelope's village, and not as tall. Its sides were not as steep, making the trail to the top easier to climb, but harder to defend. The travelers were observed long before they started up the footpath, and a crowd of villagers had gathered at the trail's end to greet them.

The man who stepped forward to grip Father's arms was short and muscular, and appeared to be about Father's age. He wore a cotton garment at his waist that reached to his knees. It was blue except for four parallel black stripes at the center. Running Antelope recognized him as the village chief and father of his friend Growing Reed. "Welcome to our village, my brother!" the chief said to Father. Then, with open arms extended toward the others, he called out, "We welcome you, our brothers!"

Running Antelope found himself surrounded by friendly villagers adding their own greetings to those of their chief. From behind, someone slapped him hard on the shoulder. He turned, raising his hands to protect himself from further blows, only to stare into the grinning face of his friend.

"I am happy to see you again, big brother!" Growing Reed shouted above the crowd's noise, his dark eyes sparkling with joy.

"Ai, little brother!" Running Antelope responded, laughing at the way they referred to each other. He had the same number of summers as Growing Reed, but was taller by four fingers. Growing Reed was short and stocky like his father.

"You look the same as when you came here before, big brother!"

14

"So do you, little brother!" They both laughed. "Are you better now with bow and arrow, or are the crows still safe when your arrows fly?"

"Ai, big brother! To be safe when your arrows fly, I will stand in front of you!" They both laughed again.

The friendly crowd escorted the visitors to a nearby kiva. "This is the kiva of the Bow Clan," Growing Reed pointed out. "You know that my father is clan chief. He will see to the needs of your father and his companions here. They will talk and pray, and smoke the pipe. Later they will eat food and rest for the night." Running Antelope nodded his understanding. "You and I can go to my mother's house and do the same things...except no smoking the pipe," he coughed before grinning broadly. "We can go to the fields and hunt rabbits, instead." The two friends walked on, passing a second kiva before turning toward a row of houses. "That is the kiva of the Reed Clan, and ahead of us is where I live."

"It all looks as I remember it. I am happy to be in your village again, little brother!"

Growing Reed lived with his parents and younger sister in a single-room dwelling constructed in a similar manner as Running Antelope's home. A ladder provided access to the flat roof of cottonwood beams and branches where Growing Reed slept at night. Much of the family's food preparation was done in an area just outside the dwelling's only doorway. It was there that Growing Reed's mother and sister were kneeling on folded cotton blankets, each in front of a large flat stone. They were grinding blue corn with rounded, hand-held stones, and singing a grinding song. The boys approached them, pausing not far away to listen to the words and sweet tones.

Oh, Corn Mother,
Thank you for your gifts.
This corn is for our piki.
Piki is the perfect food.

Growing Reed spoke when the singing stopped. "My mother! See my friend Running Antelope! He has come to our village again!"

Mother looked up from her work and smiled. She was a short-legged, round woman wrapped in a blue cotton blanket that was knotted over the left shoulder, leaving her right arm and shoulder bare. The garment was tied at the waist with an embroidered belt. "We heard of your arrival, Running Antelope. You are welcome in our home."

"Thank you. I am happy to be here."

"And you know my sister Standing Blossom. She was smaller when you last came here. She now has twelve summers."

Standing Blossom looked at Running Antelope with dark, shining eyes. Her black hair was wound into two tight buds, one on each side of her head. A blanket like her mother's hid her slender figure. She offered a brief, shy smile when Running Antelope greeted her, but said nothing.

Mother returned to her grinding. "There is piki to eat. Offer some to Running Antelope. Then you can show him how you keep the rats from eating our corn."

И И И

As Sun Father descended toward its western kiva, the two young hunters trudged back up the footpath to the safety of the village. There were others on the trail—men and boys who had been cultivating the soil around corn and squash, beans and melons, cotton and gourds—and women and girls carrying the day's last load of spring water in large, clay vessels strapped to their backs or foreheads. The boys were tired, especially Running Antelope. Both were hungry. Each carried a rabbit killed with his throwing stick, gifts for Growing Reed's mother to compensate for the lack of rat-tail trophies.

It was dusk when they reached home. "There is stew waiting for you," said Mother, gratefully accepting the rabbits. Growing Reed picked up the warm bowl and carried it with him as he and Running Antelope climbed the ladder to the rooftop where Mother had spread rabbitskin blankets.

"Your mother makes good stew," said Running Antelope after tasting the well-cooked mixture of corn kernels, beans, and pieces of rabbit meat in thick gravy of cornmeal and water. He licked his fingers and then helped himself to more. Growing Reed nodded in agreement, his mouth full. The two friends emptied the bowl and continued to sit cross-legged, facing the darkening western sky. For a while, only the shrill cries of skimming nighthawks broke the silence.

Growing Reed spoke softly, "Sun Father rests now."

"Yes. Soon he will begin his journey across the world below."

"Sleep well, big brother. We will awaken to greet him when he returns."

Running Antelope lay back on the rabbitskin blanket, taking one last look at the star-filled sky. "Sleep well, little brother."

Distant voices were interrupting Running Antelope's dream when Growing Reed's urgent whispers roused him from sleep "Wake up, big brother! Wake up!"

"What is happening, little brother?" Running Antelope grumbled, rising up on his forearms. "It is still night!"

"Someone is shouting! Many people are shouting! Over there near the kivas!"

Running Antelope sat up and listened. "I hear the voices! It must be an attack on the village! Old Enemies! We must go there and help our fathers!"

The boys scrambled down the ladder, picked up their bows, quivers, and rabbit sticks, and raced toward the kivas. The early morning's half-moon bathed the mesa and its surroundings in soft light. "Over there, past the Bow kiva!" Growing Reed called out, his voice tense. A large group of villagers had gathered along the mesa's edge, talking excitedly among themselves and calling for others to join them as they gazed down at the desert floor.

"There is my father!" cried Growing Reed, as the two slowed to a walk, "And your father, too!" Both fathers were speaking with men around them while glancing frequently over the mesa's edge, expressions of dismay and disbelief on their faces.

Running Antelope dropped to his knees and crawled over to the edge. "Ai!" he gasped, his widening eyes fixed on the unfolding scene below. A band of many strangers was making camp at the base of the mesa. "They have hair on their faces...and their skin is white!"

"Ai!" Growing Reed shuddered. "Their headdresses and the clothes on their chests shine in the moon's light! And their animals! What animals are those?"

"They are like dogs of great size! And look! See how they paw at the ground and blow smoke from their noses when they make sounds!"

"There is one that is part man!" Growing Reed cried, his voice quivering. He pointed to one of the creatures that looked to be both animal and man. "The upper part of a white man's body has grown up from the back of the great dog!"

The crowd of men, women, and children on both sides of the boys gasped loudly in astonishment when the animal-man began to split in two. Running Antelope swallowed hard. "The man part has legs of its own!" In the faint light of early dawn, he watched with overwhelming feelings of wonder and fear as the man part slid to the ground and walked about with the other men. "What am I looking at?" he cried softly. "What are my eyes seeing?"

2

As Sun Father became visible, the villagers grew increasingly alarmed about the strange men and fearsome animals now confronting them, and many expressed their feelings in prayer. Running Antelope stood with them on the mesa's edge, his prayer adding strength to all that were uttered. "Oh, Great Power," he whispered, his voice filled with emotion. "Thank you for keeping us! I know I must keep my thoughts right and good." He swallowed hard, his eyes tightly closed. "I will not wish harm to the men with white faces. I will not wish harm to their animals that frighten me. Thoughts that are right and good will keep us all safe. Thank you, Great Power, that I know this." He took a handful of cornmeal from a basket tray passed to him, handed the tray to Growing Reed, and then tossed the offering toward the rising sun. He was watching its cloud drift away when Father walked up from behind and touched his shoulder.

"My son, I am going with the warriors to meet the men below." His voice was quiet, but firm. "Big Bull Snake and Two Snakes will go with me. So will Two Horns Lowered. You are to stay here with your friend."

"I want to go with you, my father!" Running Antelope appealed anxiously, picking up his weapons. "I have my bow and club!"

Father hesitated as he looked around at the men leaving the mesa's edge. Older boys were leaving, too. He turned again to Running Antelope. "Stay far behind us," he said solemnly before walking away in the direction of the Bow kiva.

א א א

Running Antelope watched silently as the warriors of the village filed out of the two kivas and formed a single line behind a tall, broad-shouldered man standing beside Growing Reed's father. The man was armed with only a stone-head ax.

"That is the war chief next to my father".

The warriors wore caps made from the skins of mountain lions, with eagle feathers attached. Many carried bows, with full quivers of arrows slung over their shoulders. Others had clubs and carried shields of woven reeds. At the war chief's command, they followed the two leaders toward the mesa's edge. As they proceeded down the footpath, all began to sing. The expressions on their sun-darkened faces were grave, and their voices were deep and strong.

"I have heard that singing before," Growing Reed spoke again. "They sing to make themselves brave."

"Yes," agreed Running Antelope grimly. "That is singing I must learn."

"I, also!"

The two friends joined the older boys who had begun to follow the warriors down the footpath. Running Antelope glanced frequently at the strangers moving about on the broad stretch of rocky terrain between the mesa's base and the nearest patches of corn. "The white-faces see the warriors coming...and many are climbing on the backs of their great dogs!"

"Look there...walking out in front of the great dogs! I see men with dark faces like ours...one...two...three of them! They are dressed like the A:shiwi from Hawikú!"

On the desert floor, the strangers had arranged themselves in two lines facing the mesa. Men on the backs of their huge animals formed the longer line. The shorter line, off to its right, consisted of men on foot carrying weapons Running Antelope could not identify. The three A:shiwi stood in front of the longer line talking with their hands to the warriors coming off the footpath. Next to them, mounted on one of the animals, was a stranger whose headpiece glittered golden as the sun, unlike the others whose headpieces were tarnished silver, more like the moon.

As the warriors left the footpath, they formed a line facing the strangers with their two chiefs standing opposite the A:shiwi. The group of older boys spread out behind the line. Running Antelope and Growing Reed broke away from them, sprinting to a position near the shorter line of strangers. "We can see better from here," panted Running Antelope, crouching behind a chest-high boulder, "And we can let arrows fly without hitting our warriors." Raising their eyes over the top of the boulder, they got their first close up look at the strangers. "The white-faces standing near us are so tall! And they carry weapons I have never seen!"

"Some are holding short bows...but I do not see arrows!"

"What are those big sticks some carry on one shoulder? They are as long as a man! How are they used?"

"Look at that man standing alone behind the others! He has no weapon, and he wears a cross of peace tied to his waist! Have these white-faces come in peace?"

"I see him, little brother! He is not dressed like the others. His long robe reaches to his ankles. Could he be a chief?"

"Perhaps one of them, but another chief must be that white-face on the great dog in front of the others...the one whose headdress shines like Sun Father. Much talking is going on!"

"Did you see that, little brother? One of the warriors just handed the war chief a big jar!" The boys watched intently as the war chief poured cornmeal from the jar while walking the length of the line of warriors. He then returned to his position next to Growing Reed's father and spoke loudly to the stranger with the golden headpiece, making hand gestures to support his words.

"He is telling the strangers not to cross the line of sacred cornmeal!" Growing Reed said anxiously. "He does not want them in our..."

"Ayih! Little brother!" Running Antelope interrupted, the fear in his voice drowned out by the yelling of men and thudding of hoofs. Several animals had charged at the warriors opposite them. They were pulled back quickly by the men on their backs, but not before one of the warriors swung his club, striking an animal on the side of its head.

An angry voice called out from behind the shorter line of strangers, "To tell the truth, I do not know why we even came here!" It was the man wearing the long robe and the cross of peace speaking in a language Running Antelope did not understand. As if the man's words were a signal, both lines of strangers shouted, "SANTIAGO!" and charged at the warriors.

Running Antelope watched, terrified, as the warriors turned about and ran in panic. Many were knocked to the ground by the powerful animals. The footpath was soon filled with fleeing warriors and the boys who had come down to help them—all seeking the safety of their village. The two friends huddled in fear behind the boulder, not wanting to see any more. Clouds of dust swept past them, as did the cries of men. The boys closed their eyes and put hands over their ears until the sounds gradually faded away. Then, for a while, there was silence.

ℵ ℵ ℵ

Running Antelope heard the animal approaching before he saw it. He did not want to see it, but he forced himself to peek between fingers of his hands now covering his face. He moaned, and then shuddered, "A white-face is looking at us from the back of his giant dog!" His voice was a frightened whisper. "He is pointing at us with a long spear!"

"I see him!" whimpered Growing Reed, his body trembling. "His spear is as long as two men!"

"See his face, little brother! It is angry! And see his long scar!"

The stranger's gray eyes were fixed on the two boys, an expression of disgust on his face. A jagged scar began on his right cheek just above his dark beard. It ran upward across the bridge of his nose to the left side of his forehead where it disappeared under the dull-gray helmet he wore. He scowled when he spoke to them in his language, "You are afraid of my lance, young *moquis*? Or my horse? Or both? You should have run away with the others!" He lifted his lance so that it pointed straight up before returning its butt end to the leather holder near his right stirrup. Spurring his horse lightly, he rode off to rejoin the other cavalrymen, a scowl still on his face.

A feeling of relief washed over Running Antelope. He remained sitting with his back against the boulder, the sun-baked mesa in front of him. Movement to his left caught the corner of his eye. "Little brother!" he cried out, nudging Growing Reed with his elbow. "Our people are returning!" The two gazed unbelievingly at the procession coming down the footpath. There were men, women, and children—the entire village—walking slowly, quietly down the zigzagging trail. Running Antelope stood up and peeked over the top of the boulder to see the reaction of the strangers. Most of the riders had dismounted from their horses and were standing around in small groups watching the villagers advance.

"I see our fathers!" said Growing Reed, relief in his voice and the hint of a smile on his face. "We should be with them!"

"Ai, little brother! See if you can keep up with me!"

The two raced the short distance to the villagers, joining their fathers at the head of the orderly crowd. Running Antelope greeted his father as he fell in beside him. Then, looking up, he asked, "My father, who are these men with white faces and giant dogs?"

They took several steps before Father replied. "They are called Spaniards. They have great power and have killed many who live in Hawikú. We are told this by their guides." He had started his words in a strong voice, but ended them in a whisper.

Running Antelope felt fear, not only from his father's words, but also from the look of helplessness on his face. "What are we to do, my father?" he asked, softly.

"We are taking them gifts. The people of Kawaioukuh have brought corn and cornmeal, cloth made from their cotton, many soft skins, and several young hawks. We will tell them that we want peace...that we want to be friends."

They continued on without speaking. Only the sounds of children crying and women moaning reached their ears. Running Antelope trembled when he heard a woman behind him tearfully ask, "Are the giant dogs going to eat us?" He had pictured the same possibility in his own mind.

Growing Reed's father raised his arm and the procession stopped about ten paces from where the Spaniards stood. He then held out both hands and formed a cross with the fingers closest to his thumbs. As the villagers spread out to face the strange men, many made the same sign of peace.

Running Antelope gave a soft sigh of relief when the three A:shiwi guides stepped forward and formed crosses with their fingers. He listened with eyes moist with tears as Growing Reed's father spoke of peace, friendship, and surrender. Two of the Spaniards stepped over to the guides and received the message in translation, with sign language used more than words. Running Antelope recognized the two as the stranger chiefs he and Growing Reed had identified—one wearing a golden headdress, the other a cross of peace hanging from his robe's waistcord. The stranger chiefs nodded their heads as if in agreement, so Growing Reed's father continued. He asked his people to present their gifts by laying them at the feet of the Spaniards. When this was done, he spoke again, inviting the Spaniards to come up to the village to talk and eat, and also to trade.

Running Antelope stayed close to his father's side. After the peace-making ended, he walked with him up the footpath once again. This time, Spaniards walked behind them, talking among themselves and laughing now and then—loudly—as if something humorous was happening. It had been many summers since he gripped his father's hand as they walked. He wanted to do that now, but he did not.

3

The southern part of the huge mesa was in the form of a lizard's head. The snout was the mesa's southern tip, and its lower jaw was the southeastern side where Kawaioukuh was located. The village was home to nineteen Hópitu families representing the Bow and Reed Clans. Their kivas, centers of village life, had been dug as close to the mesa's edge as possible, and only a few steps from the footpath leading to the desert floor. Their stone and mortar houses were clustered in threes and fours near the kivas. Two main pathways of sand and exposed sandstone separated the structures, and were about as wide as the length of three men.

The Spaniards, numbering about thirty, wandered about the village looking inside the dwellings and sharing their observations among themselves. The villagers stood along the pathways watching apprehensively.

"Prepare food for the visitors! Prepare food!" the village chief shouted, rushing about anxiously. "Show them what you have to trade! Get out pottery and blankets! Get out skins and cloth! Get out gourds and corn!" By the time he reached the Bow kiva, beads of sweat were dripping from his face. Running Antelope was standing there with his father and uncle. Growing Reed was there, too, as were Big Bull Snake and Two Snakes. "These Spaniards think we have gold!" the chief fumed. "I told them that there is no gold here! Now they can see for themselves!"

Big Bull Snake stepped forward, his broad forehead wrinkled in thought. "Perhaps you could tell them of the Great Red River to the west where giant men live. Tell them they might find gold there."

"The giant men could pick up a Spaniard's animal and throw it to the ground!" Two Snakes added with a sneer. "I would like to see that!"

"Telling them of the Great Red River might get them to leave," the chief said softly, a look of hope on his face.

As the men continued to talk, Growing Reed motioned to Running Antelope. "I want to see my mother," he whispered, as the two stepped away. "I want to know that she is safe." The boys paused, allowing a group of Spaniards to walk by in the opposite direction. They studied them with great interest. "Each white-face wears clothes over all of his body!" Growing Reed remarked, noting the high leather boots worn with trousers that flared above the knees, and the sweat-stained, long-sleeve shirts worn under steel vests. "They must feel Sun Father's warmth much more than we do."

"I would never wear so many clothes," responded Running Antelope, shaking his head. "I would feel like piki coming off a hot stone!"

"Oh-ee-e! You would have smoke pouring from your ears!"

"Look at the weapon each one has at his waist, little brother." Both boys took on a more serious manner. "Is that a long knife or a short spear?"

"It has a handle like a knife, big brother, so it must not be thrown."

"Its blade is long and thin, and comes to a sharp point! Do you think they stick them into people like we pretend to do with yucca blades?"

Growing Reed's attention was distracted before he could answer. "That white-face over there has been inside the Reed kiva!" he exploded, angrily. He was looking at a Spaniard whose helmeted head had just popped up from the kiva's entrance hole. "YOU ARE NOT TO BE IN THERE!" he shouted at the man. "THAT IS A SACRED PLACE!"

The Spaniard stepped from the ladder to the roof with only a glance in Growing Reed's direction.

"He does not understand you, little brother. If he did, he would want to stick you with his blade for yelling at him."

"I do not like them being here!" Growing Reed grumbled.

"Little brother! Look! There are more of them at your house!"

Three bearded Spaniards, each with a musket, were standing outside the flat-roofed dwelling waiting for Growing Reed's mother to serve them stew from a large, smoke-blackened cooking pot. Standing Blossom stood next to her holding a stack of piki bread, a distressed look on her face. Using a gourd ladle, Mother filled a bowl with the thick, warm mixture and handed it to the Spaniard closest to her. Standing Blossom held out some of the piki, her eyes lowered and her hand trembling. The man laughed as he took the bread, then moved out of the way of his companions.

Mother was filling a second bowl when the two boys walked up to her. Without looking away from her task, she spoke to Growing Reed. "My son, you and Running Antelope take your sister away from here." She spoke softly, but with a sternness that surprised both boys. "Go to where the corn grows. You can play, or send arrows at crows...whatever you want." She handed the bowl to the next Spaniard, and then looked up at both boys with eyes narrowed. "You are not to return to our village until these men have gone!"

"Yes, my mother," Growing Reed answered softly without looking at the Spaniards. Catching his sister's eye, he motioned for her to come with him. Standing Blossom started to follow, then stopped to hand the remaining piki to her mother.

"No, you keep that for the three of you. I will get more."

"Yes, my mother," Standing Blossom whispered, holding back tears. She then turned and followed her brother and Running Antelope away from the house, ignoring the questioning looks of the three soldiers.

"We can walk around the village and not have to look at any more hairy white faces!" Growing Reed said bitterly. He continued to lead the way, taking a route that circled to the north and east around the village.

The three glanced frequently off to their right. "Little brother, do you see our fathers?" Running Antelope called ahead.

"We cannot see the Bow kiva because of the houses, big brother! That is where they must be!"

The three reached the mesa's edge northeast of the village. "I know another way down," Growing Reed called out, stopping to wait for his sister and Running Antelope to catch up. "It is a steep path...not too steep to go down, but too steep to come up." He turned and began his descent, moving cautiously, using short steps, sliding here and there down the faint, zigzagging trail.

Running Antelope waited for Standing Blossom to go ahead of him, but she made no move to follow her brother. "It is too steep for me!" she called out to Growing Reed. She looked back at Running Antelope, a troubled expression on her face. "I will fall!"

"We can walk slowly," he assured her, taking her hand.

She looked again at him, and then looked away, redness coloring her cheeks. Taking a deep breath, she said, "I will try."

Running Antelope stayed beside her for support as she duplicated his steps. They moved slowly, pausing frequently to assess the next part of the trail. When they were a little more than halfway down, the trail broadened and the degree of slope lessened. They increased their speed to a fast walk until their momentum forced them to run as the trail emptied onto the desert floor. They were both laughing when they caught up with Growing Reed.

"See where they left their great dogs," Growing Reed said, looking toward the campsite and the tethered horses nearby. "I count ten and eight of the animals."

"We will have to go around them to reach the corn, little brother."

"We can do that, or we can go right by them and get a closer look."

"I think we should go around them," said Standing Blossom, a look of concern returning to her face, "far around them!"

"They are tied to something so they are not going to attack us, my sister. What do you think, big brother? Shall we take a closer look?"

"We can get a little closer, but I do not want your sister to be frightened."

"Then let us walk to the left of them. My sister, you tell us when we are too close. Then we will move away." The three continued in the direction of the animals, their shadows on the rocky terrain getting shorter as Sun Father approached his midday position.

"A white-face just came out from behind the great dogs!" warned Running Antelope, his eyes squinting from the sun's brightness. "Do you see him, little brother?"

"I see him! He carries a long stick weapon on his shoulder, and he is looking at us!"

"We should stop now!" insisted Standing Blossom. "We are too close! We do not know what that man will do!"

"Listen!" Running Antelope said sharply, turning to gaze back at the mesa. "Listen to the sounds from the village!" They stood motionless, eyes fixed on the mesa top, then widening in disbelief.

"I hear yelling and screaming...terrible screaming!" Standing Blossom gasped, her eyes filling with tears.

"And sounds of thunder! Do you hear them, big brother?"

"Yes, I hear them! I do not know what causes them! But the screams! Something bad is happening!"

"Hai!" cried Growing Reed, turning again in the direction of the tethered animals. "The white-face by the great dogs is shouting at us...and he is pointing his stick weapon at us!" The three stared at the Spaniard in bewilderment as his musket's powder charge flashed, followed instantly by its thunderous clap. The musket ball whined past them like an angry hornet.

"Run!" shouted Growing Reed, ducking low and racing toward the patches of corn.

Running Antelope grabbed Standing Blossom's hand and pulled her with him as he followed Growing Reed. "Stay with me!" he cried. They ran past the corn and cotton patches, their feet flying over sandy soil and desert grass. Another thunderclap frightened them into an even greater burst of speed as a musket ball kicked up a spray of sand and rock particles near them.

"We can hide in the streambed!" Growing Reed called out. "Over here!" The dry, shallow streambed he leaped into was about as wide as the length of two men, and was lined with desert plants growing along its banks. He skidded to a stop in soft sand and fell to his hands and knees behind a row of shoulder-high mesquite bushes. Running Antelope and Standing Blossom slid to a stop next to him. They huddled there breathing heavily, hearts pounding, their ears alert to more sounds of thunder.

И И И

It was long after he caught his breath when Running Antelope stood up to peer cautiously over the spiny branches of the mesquite. "The white-face with the stick weapon still stands near the great dogs," he said softly. "His back is to us. He is looking toward the village."

Growing Reed stood up beside him and gazed at the mesa, his eyes blinking against the glare of sunlight. "There is smoke coming from the village," he said, his voice choked with emotion.

"I see it, little brother. I see it." Running Antelope sighed, a feeling of helplessness growing within him.

"Big Brother! Look! The white-faces are coming down the footpath! They are walking as if they are in no hurry!"

"That is a bad sign. Our warriors should be sending arrows after them."

Standing Blossom rose to her feet, her eyes taking in the scene. "What has happened to our village? What has happened to our mother and father?"

The three stood together in the streambed, arms about each other, watching the Spaniards saddle horses and break camp. They continued to gaze in silence as those who mounted the animals pointed their long lances skyward and started off in a column of pairs toward the southeast. The cavalrymen held their horses to a slow pace, allowing those who followed on foot to keep up—the soldiers with the stick weapons—the A:shiwi guides—and the one with the cross of peace tied at the waist of his long robe.

4

Running Antelope led the way out of the streambed, took another long look toward the southeast, and then moved at a fast trot in the direction of the village. Growing Reed and Standing Blossom were right behind him. From the corn patches, they headed across the campsite the Spaniards had vacated and over the rocky ground where the war chief's line of sacred cornmeal was still visible. They slowed to a walk upon reaching the footpath at the base of the mesa.

"The white-faces are far away now!" Growing Reed announced, taking a deep breath. "Their great dogs get smaller each time I look."

"I hope they never return!" Standing Blossom stated emphatically. "They frighten me...and I am afraid for our village...our people!"

The smell of smoke was strong as they reached the top of the footpath. Cottonwood roof beams were smoldering in both kivas and in several houses. The occasional crackling of burning wood was the only sound to be heard.

Growing Reed looked to his left and his face paled. "There are bodies near the Bow kiva!" he said just above a whisper, his voice tense.

"There are many bodies there!" Running Antelope gasped as the three walked haltingly into the village.

"Is there no one left alive?" Standing Blossom cried, tears streaming down her face.

"Ayih! Ayih!" Growing Reed wailed as they moved closer to the kiva. "Ayih! Our father is there!"

"My father...is there, too!" Running Antelope moaned, his voice quivering.

All three wept softly as they viewed the lifeless forms of their fathers lying on the blood soaked ground. They wrapped their arms around each other and let the tears flow. "The breath-bodies of our fathers are now free to follow Sun Father," Running Antelope whispered to his friends. "They will pass downward through the *sipápuni* to the world below where they will have new birth."

Growing Reed cleared his throat, and then added, "Their spirits will be with the Cloud People and they will visit us to bring rain for our corn."

"And they...will be...with the Katsinam...and will come to our village... to dance for us," Standing Blossom sobbed, trying to control her trembling voice.

Running Antelope looked about at other fallen figures. "Little brother," he called softly. "My father's clan brother lies next to the kiva." He nodded toward the body of Big Bull Snake. "And I see the war chief near him."

Growing Reed walked over to the two forms. He nodded his head slowly and wiped his eyes with both hands. "Yes, big brother," he sighed. "Their breath-bodies have left through their open mouths."

"My brothers!" Standing Blossom called out anxiously. "We must find our mother!" Without another word said, the three moved quickly toward the nearest row of dwellings. They passed more fallen villagers, including women, and paused long enough to make sure that Mother was not one of them.

Growing Reed was the first to see her. He came to a stop a few steps from the grinding stones that had occupied so much of her life. He held out his arms for the others to stop with him. "Our mother is protecting her home," he said solemnly, his voice shaking.

Standing Blossom covered her face with both hands and wept, her grief overwhelming her. Running Antelope placed his hand on her shoulder and she turned to him and let him hold her. Mother's body lay at the entrance to the dwelling, turned as if to face those who killed her. The blue cotton blanket she wore was blood red over her heart. Behind her, smoldering cottonwood and pieces of mortar from the collapsed roof filled the room.

With Running Antelope's help, Growing Reed moved his mother beyond the grinding stones and covered her with the blanket she had used so often as a cushion for her knees. "We will come back for you, my mother," he sobbed. "But first we must see if there is anyone still living."

The three wandered through the rest of the village, only to find additional bodies and more destruction. "There are no white-face bodies!" Growing Reed snapped angrily, the reddish-brown skin of his broad face turning a darker red. "Why is that so, big brother? I have counted all of my fingers two times. There are that many bodies of our people here, but no white-faces!"

Running Antelope did not respond immediately. His attention was focused a few steps away. "Here is one more, little brother. It is my uncle!" He walked up to the body of Two Horns Lowered. "He lies here with an empty bow in his hand." Then, seeing the buckskin quiver still strapped to his uncle's back, he added, "And only a few arrows remain."

"My brothers!" Standing Blossom called out. "People are coming!" She was looking to the north where the mesa broadens into its hugeness.

"Our people are returning!" shouted Growing Reed, the beginning of a smile on his face. The villagers, less then sixty in number, were walking slowly toward them—cautiously—quietly. Most were women and children, with only a dozen or so men among them. Some waved when they recognized the three youngsters running to greet them.

Growing Reed and Standing Blossom found the loving arms of aunts and cousins. Running Antelope heard his name called and turned to see Two Snakes waving at him. They walked toward each other silently and gripped each other's arms when they met. They held on firmly, seeing in the other's eyes the pain they both felt.

The villagers broke up into family and neighbor groups and entered the area of death and destruction. Tears flowed freely, then cries and wails filled the air as the bodies of loved ones were discovered.

И И И

The heat of the day had given way to the coolness of early evening when Running Antelope and Two Snakes strolled over to the Bow kiva to talk. They had finished helping villagers carry the dead to the homes of family. The bodies had been laid on the ground outside, bent into squatting positions, and wrapped in blankets to await preparation for burial. As Growing Reed approached them, Running Antelope called to him solemnly, "Little brother! You should hear this! Two Snakes is telling me that the killing began here where we are standing." He paused, a look of anguish in his eyes as his friend joined them. "He will tell you what he was explaining to me."

Two Snakes shifted his feet and nodded toward the kivas. "Their chief...the one who covers his head with gold...sent men into both kivas. He was angry because no gold had been found. Your father," he nodded at Growing Reed, "showed his own anger when we all heard sounds from the kivas that told us that these sacred places were being destroyed. He shouted at the Spaniard chief telling him to order his men to come out. That is when a white-face holding a stick weapon walked over to your father and clubbed him, knocking him to the ground. His head was bleeding...and he did not move."

Two Snakes paused and bowed his head, shaking it slowly from side to side. Growing Reed's eyes were fixed on him, and he asked gravely—insistently, "What happened next?"

Two Snakes looked up, his face flushed, his eyes narrowed. "Running Antelope's father stepped forward," he continued, his voice strained. "His hands were held out...open in friendship. He spoke words urging calmness and peace." Running Antelope felt a sickness in his stomach, fearing what would be said next as Two Snakes looked at him with sorrowful eyes.

"Another Spaniard rushed in and stabbed him with his long knife! It went all the way through his body! I could see death come to his eyes quickly." Two Snakes paused again, then spoke just above a whisper, "My brother...Big Bull Snake...raised his staff to strike this white-face...and thunder sounded like I have never heard! It came from the stick weapon, followed by much smoke! My brother fell backward to the ground with a dark hole in his chest!" His voice had risen in anger, and his face was wet with tears. "Then that ugly Spaniard with the long knife still in his hand reached down and stabbed him!"

Running Antelope could no longer listen. He turned and walked away, deep in his own thoughts. He headed for the far side of the mesa's tip where beyond he could see Sun Father approaching his western kiva. He imagined his own father's breath-body already there, ready to follow Sun Father to the lower world where all of his people had their beginning. He did not hear Two Snakes tell of Two Horns Lowered and himself backing away from the violence and drawing arrows from their quivers. "I sent my arrow flying at the Spaniard with the long knife. I wanted to hit the long scar that crossed his ugly face...but my arrow struck him near his heart and bounced off! He was not harmed! I backed away further and heard thunder all around me! I started to run! Others ran with me! We hid among rocks far from the village!"

Two Snakes stopped to calm himself and then slumped dejectedly to the ground, his arms folded on bended knees. He breathed deeply, resting his forehead on his arms, then said with a sigh, "I did not know what happened to Two Horns Lowered."

5

Running Antelope was awakened before dawn by the smell of death all around him. He and the others had slept outside the undamaged house of one of the aunts—the oldest sister of Growing Reed's father. As the others were stirring, he walked in the darkness to the edge of the mesa. Standing there silently, he looked toward the east, thoughts of his father on his mind. He watched as white dawn arrived and slowly changed to yellow dawn. As the sun became visible on the horizon, he whispered his prayer. "Oh, Sun Father, I thank Great Power for you. I thank Great Power for sending my father's breath-body with you to the underworld where he will wake up and find new life. I thank Great Power that I know to let sad thoughts leave me, and evil thoughts, too. I want a heart that is happy and good. I am happy to greet you, Sun Father."

His friends soon joined him and he was passed a basket tray of cornmeal. After taking a handful, he tossed it in front of him and watched its cloud drift out of sight. When the others were ready, he turned and walked with them back to Aunt's dwelling.

И И И

Aunt took charge of burial preparations for Running Antelope's father, uncle, and Big Bull Snake, as well as for the father and mother of Growing Reed and Standing Blossom. The blanket-wrapped bodies had been placed beyond her outdoor cooking fire, awaiting daylight.

"She and my younger aunt will begin with my father," Growing Reed said knowingly after he and Running Antelope returned with a freshly cut yucca root and stems. Aunt cut off some root and shredded it. She then pounded it with a stone on a flat rock to get its liquid. "They will wash his hair with yucca suds. Then his face and hands. Standing Blossom will learn from them." Running Antelope nodded. He knew of the procedure, but had never taken part in it.

The two brought fresh water and poured it into large washing bowls, as they were told, until each of the dead was washed. They helped raise each body to a sitting position so Aunt could arrange its hair.

While Standing Blossom helped her aunts dress Mother in a fresh blanket and belt, the boys collected prayer feathers from inside the dwelling. Then they watched as the women rubbed cornmeal over the chief's face and fitted over it a cotton mask with holes for eyes and mouth. "The mask will be like a cloud to hide my father's face when he returns to bring rain for our corn," Growing Reed quietly observed.

"The same will be true for my father," Running Antelope agreed, as the women repeated the process with the others.

The boys helped the women fill each lifeless hand with cornmeal and tie the fingers closed with split yucca stems. Then they helped fasten prayer feathers to hands, feet, and hair. When this was done, Aunt offered Growing Reed a basket tray of cornmeal. "Take some and sprinkle it over my brother... your father." When Growing Reed had done so, she spoke directly to his father. "My brother, your life here is finished. You will soon go to your new home where you will be happy. You have been known here as Arrows Go Far, the chief of our village. You will leave that name here with your body. You will have a new name for your new home. That name will be..." She did not finish.

"My father's new name will not be spoken here," Growing Reed said, his voice firm but quiet. "He knows the name and will take it with him."

Aunt then offered the basket tray to Standing Blossom. "Sprinkle cornmeal over your mother." When this was done, she continued, "Stand Up Gracefully, your life here is finished. You will soon go to your new home with a new name. That name will be..."

Standing Blossom knelt beside her mother's body, her chest heaving as she cried between words, "My mother...I want you...to stay with me! I am lost...without you! I...do not know what to do!" She remained there on her knees, crying softly as Aunt turned to Running Antelope.

"Sprinkle cornmeal over your father and uncle." Running Antelope fought back tears as he did so. Aunt spoke louder as she addressed the two. "Many Rattles and Two Horns Lowered! Your lives here have ended! You will take new names with you to your new home. Your names will be..."

Running Antelope wiped his eyes and cleared his throat. "My father...I will miss you! Our lives...will be hard without you. Remember us!" he sobbed.

"I hope you will visit us often!" He then turned to Two Horns Lowered. "My uncle...you have been like a brother. I will miss you! We all will miss you!"

Aunt motioned to Two Snakes to take some cornmeal. "Sprinkle some over your brother." The young man stepped forward stiffly, his thin face grief-stricken, his dark eyes filled with anger. He hesitated, as if to say something, then scattered the cornmeal on Big Bull Snake's body. "Big Bull Snake!" Aunt spoke again. "Your life in this world is over. Soon you will go to your new home in the world below. You will no longer need the name Big Bull Snake. Your new name will be..."

Two Snakes' breathing had become heavy and his face was contorted in anguish. "My brother!" he wailed. "You are father and brother to me!" He pounded his chest with both fists. "Your death has turned my heart to stone! I must breathe vengeance on those who did this to you! Their blood for your blood!" He turned away and stood by himself, fists still clenched. "Their blood for your blood!" he said again, bitterly.

ᴎ ᴎ ᴎ

Sun Father was midway on his course when Running Antelope, Growing Reed, and Two Snakes re-wrapped the bodies in blankets and bound them with split yucca stems. They first carried Big Bull Snake and Two Horns Lowered to the burial ground, and then returned for the other three. Standing Blossom carried five sticks of greasewood, each as long as a man's arm. The two aunts carried digging sticks, a cloth sack of cornmeal, five water gourds, and five small bowls containing cornmeal mush and piki bread.

The burial ground was northeast of the village along a low ridge. The ridge curved to the north, providing a gentle eastern slope of sandy soil for graves to be dug. Several groups of villagers were already burying their dead. "Let us dig holes along here as far apart as a man's length," suggested Two Snakes. The boys watched as he marked five large circles in the dirt with a digging stick, stepping off two paces between them. "When the holes are deep enough, I will show you how to dig the caves."

The three worked steadily with digging sticks and hands until the holes were dug, each as deep as the length of a man's leg. "The cave in each hole must be on this side," Two Snakes said, pointing with his digging stick at the west side of the hole nearest him. "It must be large enough for the body to sit in with legs folded, facing the hole and each new dawn." He climbed into the hole and began to gouge the outline of a cave with his stick. The boys watched briefly, and then went back to work.

When all five caves were hollowed out, Aunt sprinkled cornmeal where each body would sit. "The houses are ready," she announced softly, a deep sadness in her dark, wrinkled face. They all helped lower the bodies into the holes. Each body was gently pressed back into its cave in a squatting position facing east. Large flat stones were used to cover the caves, and cornmeal was sprinkled on the stones.

Aunt spoke softly again, "The soil can be put back now." They all responded by dropping handfuls of the fresh dirt back into the holes, packing it with their feet, and smoothing the resulting mounds with their hands. "We must cover the mounds with piles of stones," she said with more strength in her voice. "We do not want coyotes digging here."

When stones were in place on all five mounds, Aunt handed a greasewood stick to each of the others. "Here are the ladders for the spirits to climb. Stick one in each mound. Place food and water beside it. Then we will leave."

И И И

As soon as they returned to Aunt's dwelling, she stirred up the coals of the outdoor fire and started water to boil in a large pot. While the others waited, she added several stubby juniper branches to the pot. When the branches had boiled to her satisfaction, she poured some of the water into a pottery bowl. "We must wash ourselves of any evil."

When it was his turn, Running Antelope washed his hands, arms, and face. Aunt washed his back for him, as she was doing for the others.

Aunt bathed herself last, then emptied the bowl and broke it. "This bowl cannot be used again." Turning to Growing Reed she said, "Get some more juniper from inside and put it on the coals. Bring us a blanket, as well. We must now use smoke to rid ourselves of any remaining evil."

After Growing Reed carried out his instructions and the wood had started to burn, they all stood under the blanket next to the fire. Juniper smoke swirled around them. They turned their bodies as if to bathe in it, eyes watering, coughing. When Aunt decided to stop, she gathered in the blanket and declared, "We must now wash our heads!"

И И И

"My hair smells of yucca suds and my body smells of juniper smoke!" Running Antelope complained with a grin as he sat by the fire with his friends. The heat of the day had given way to the chill of the night. Their simple meal of crumbled piki in a mush of cornmeal and water had been eaten by firelight.

36

"But big brother! You are as clean now as you were when your mother bathed you and sprinkled juniper ashes on your bottom!" Growing Reed laughed, his eyes looking to tease.

Standing Blossom laughed, too, head back, swishing her long black hair now free of the two tight buds. "I can see you in my thoughts, big brother! Even the juniper ashes!"

"Do not look too closely, little sister!" Running Antelope's grin got wider. "I would rather you think of me as the way I am now!" They all laughed. Even Two Snakes broke his somber expression with a smile.

They were still laughing when Aunt came out to the fire. "It is good that you laugh! The less you think sad thoughts, the better off you are. Unhappy thoughts can harm your body and cause trouble in your life. Keep your thoughts happy!" She waved them good night and went back inside her dwelling.

"Thank you, my aunt!" Growing Reed called to her. "Thank you for all you have done for us today!"

"Thank you, my aunt!" the other three sang out in unison.

"Does anyone else want to sleep now?" Growing Reed asked. The others shook their heads. "Then let us talk and laugh some more. It will be good for us!"

И И И

During the next two days, Running Antelope, Growing Reed, and Two Snakes hunted rabbits and protected crops from birds and rodents. Standing Blossom helped grind corn and fix meals. On the morning of the third day, the four of them returned to the burial ground carrying prayer sticks, prayer feathers, bundles of piki, and a sack of cornmeal. Others from the village were taking the same walk with similar offerings.

Upon arriving at the gravesites, they quickly set about placing the piki, prayer sticks, and prayer feathers on the piles of stones. Growing Reed poured the cornmeal on the ground, making a short trail eastward from each grave. Then they hurried away.

Two Snakes initiated the conversation as they walked back to the village. "When the dawn comes tomorrow, they will arise with haste, eat of the piki we left them, and leave on their journey with Sun Father."

"Yes," agreed Running Antelope, "and we can stand together at the edge of the village and send our prayers with them."

"And then, my younger brother," Two Snakes continued, looking at

Running Antelope, "you and I must return to our village to tell our people what has happened here."

They walked on in silence until Running Antelope spoke, his voice hopeful. "I would like you to come with us, little brother...and little sister!"

Growing Reed wrinkled his brow, his lips pressed tightly together, as if searching his thoughts for the words he wanted to say. Standing Blossom smiled, then answered first. "Thank you, big brother." She looked at Running Antelope and then looked away. "I...we...would like to come with you, but we must stay." Her voice was soft, but steady.

"We must stay with our clans!" Growing Reed said forcefully. "I must provide for my aunt as my father has done since the death of her husband. Our younger aunt has her family, but our older aunt has only my sister and me." He paused, placing his hand on Running Antelope's shoulder. "Thank you, big brother, but we must remain here and help our people survive."

6

Running Antelope walked down the footpath several paces behind Two Snakes. He did not want his voice to reveal the emotions he was feeling, so he kept silent. Leaving his two friends and the grieving village was more difficult then anything he had ever experienced. The lump in his throat still burned, and his eyes continued to water. He was sure that Growing Reed's tight grip on his arms had left bruises—and Standing Blossom's tears remained wet on his cheek. He would never wipe them off.

When they reached the desert floor, Running Antelope turned and waved. Almost all of the villagers had been on hand to see them off, and many waved in return. As patches of corn and cotton were left behind, Running Antelope noticed that Two Snakes had quickened his pace. "Are we going to run back to our village?" he called out in jest.

"We might!" came the reply. "Do you think you can keep up with me?"

Running Antelope laughed. "I know I can! You could never lose me!"

И И И

Sun Father was directly overhead when the two fast-moving travelers stopped at the top of a sandy mound to drink from their gourds and examine the surrounding terrain. Their tall, gray mesa had been in view since mid-morning, but now Running Antelope could see familiar patches of corn and cotton at its base. "We will soon be drinking water from the spring near my mother's melons," he remarked.

Two Snakes took one last swallow of water, grunted his acknowledgment of Running Antelope's observation, and strode off the mound to the northwest. With Running Antelope close behind, he soon found the faint trail and resumed his rapid pace.

И И И

Sun Father was still looking down on their heads when they approached the patches of corn farthest out from the mesa. The few men and boys working there had stopped their labor and were looking at them, using their hands to shield their eyes from the sun's glare. Running Antelope waved a greeting, but got no response. "They do not know who we are!" he said loudly.

"They will soon," Two Snakes called back. "They are being cautious until they know us."

Running Antelope waved again and shouted to a boy he recognized, "Ai! Little Thunder! I am Running Antelope!" The boy grinned and waved back. He said something to the men near him and they smiled and waved, too.

И И И

A large crowd of villagers had gathered along the eastern edge of the mesa by the time the two completed the hazardous climb up the steep and twisting footpath. Running Antelope heard calls of welcome before he could see any faces. As he took his final steps to the mesa's flat, sandstone top, he saw his mother among those nearest him. "My mother!" he cried, seeing her worried expression. He rushed to her open arms and received her hug as others stood back with puzzled looks and unanswered questions. She briefly held him at arms length and studied his tear-streaked face, then hugged him again and let her own tears flow. Leaning on him, she let him guide her as they moved slowly through the crowd toward home.

The room of his mother's house filled quickly. Running Antelope respectfully greeted his grandfather and his oldest uncle, and was embracing his sister, whose name was Large Eyes Watching, when mother touched his arm. "We will sit, my son," she said quietly, handing her daughter several woven mats to put on the floor. Then she said to the two older men, "Come sit with us, my father, and you also, my brother. We all need to hear what my son has to say."

Running Antelope sat down between his mother and sister. Completing the circle were his sister's husband Rain Walk, his uncle—mother's oldest brother Close In The Antelopes, and Grandfather—his father's father, Flute Song Pleasing. Other relatives, as well as concerned neighbors, stood shoulder-to-shoulder around the room, or peered in through the open doorway. When all were quiet, Mother squeezed Running Antelope's hand. "Please tell us what has happened, my son."

Running Antelope's description of the strangers with white, hairy faces and giant, dog-like animals brought gasps of astonishment followed by stunned silence from his audience. Flute Song Pleasing, who was the village chief, took a long breath. His dark and wrinkled face was solemn as he looked about the room and nodded to the others. "Yes, stories of these men were told to me eight or nine summers ago," he announced, his voice deep and strong. "It was said that they came from a place across the great ocean that is far to the east of us. They arrived in the lands far to the south of our village—many days walking beyond Hawikú and the other trading villages of the A:shiwi. It was first thought that they were gods." He paused, as if in deep thought, then fixed his dark eyes on Running Antelope. "But they are not. Tell us more, my grandson."

Running Antelope sipped water from a gourd that had been passed to him, and then told of the initial contact between the Kawaioukuh warriors and the Spaniards. As he spoke of the subsequent surrender and the invitation to the Spaniards to enter the village, his listeners reacted with groans and sighs.

"My friends and I were out where the corn grows when the white-faces..." he stopped as his voice trembled with emotion. He locked hands with his mother and sister. "Two Snakes later told us what happened." He paused again to control his voice. "Many people were killed by the white-faces... my father...my uncle...Big Bull Snake...my friends' father and mother...many more." He lowered his head and closed his eyes, letting tears fall where they may. Others in the room cried softly with him.

Flute Song Pleasing spoke again, his voice steady though his face showed great sorrow. "Thank you, my grandson. We must let you rest now and be with your mother and sister." He turned to Close In The Antelopes and spoke in a quiet tone, "We will meet with the other chiefs when Sun Father enters his kiva. My grandson and Two Snakes will join us."

Many embraces and thoughtful words were exchanged as people left the room. Grandfather and Uncle were the last to leave. Large Eyes Watching and Rain Walk checked on their sleeping baby while Mother and Running Antelope talked. "My son, I am sure you are hungry," Mother said, trying to keep control of her emotions. "Your sister and I will prepare food for us all." She hesitated, then turned back to look at him. "One question I must ask you, my son."

"Yes, my mother. Anything you wish."

"Were your father and Two Horns Lowered buried there the way we would have buried them here?"

Running Antelope took his mother's hands in his. "Yes, my mother," he replied. Then he smiled. "They will soon be among the Cloud People who visit us."

෴ ෴ ෴

The forty or so houses in the village had been constructed in a south-to-north double row up the middle of the narrow mesa top, allowing for a windswept pathway along both east and west sides. The village's kivas, one for each of the five clans living there, were on the eastern side, and had been dug close to the mesa's edge. They were rectangularly set so that the east-to-west path of the sun crossed their length. The pathway on this side of the mesa ran between the kivas and the row of houses.

Running Antelope and Close In The Antelopes passed by the Antelope, Snake, and Badger kivas as they walked along the pathway in the twilight of the evening. Just beyond the stretch of the mesa's edge where the villagers greet Sun Father every morning were the Flute and Rain Cloud kivas. Running Antelope did not know which one they were going to until his uncle stopped at the Flute kiva.

"This is where your grandfather is meeting with the clan chiefs. They are in there now. Follow me down the ladder. You know where to sit." Running Antelope stepped up on to the aboveground part of the structure. He followed his uncle across the flat roof to its opening and descended the ladder, briefly holding his breath as he passed through smoke from burning cedar. He remained on the raised ledge at the foot of the ladder, adjusting his eyes to the dimness. He watched his uncle step further down to the kiva's floor where the men already there greeted him. When Uncle joined their circle by sitting cross-legged on the floor, he sat down on the ledge in the same manner.

As the men talked, Running Antelope identified them in his thoughts. There was Grandfather, of course, chief of the Flute Clan as well as village chief...and Uncle, chief of the Antelope Clan. He recognized Burrow Ahead, the Badger Clan chief, and Claw Feet, the village's war chief, also from the Badger Clan. Both were fathers of friends of his. He knew Dark Cloud Coming, the chief of the Rain Cloud Clan and an old friend of his father's.

A slight movement of the ladder caused Running Antelope to look up. Two more men were entering the kiva. The first was Two Snakes. The second one he knew as Snake Moves Sideways, a friend and clan brother of his father's. *Perhaps he is here to take my father's place as clan chief*, he thought, as grief engulfed him once more.

When both men had joined the circle, Uncle picked up a ceremonial pipe and lit its sacred tobacco with a glowing ember from the fire pit. He passed the pipe to Grandfather who took several puffs before passing it to Burrow Ahead on his right. With each passing of the pipe, personal words of greeting were exchanged. When the pipe rounded the circle and reached Uncle again, he smoked before setting the pipe on the floor behind him.

The men sat quietly, heads bowed and eyes closed. Running Antelope followed their example. Thoughts of his father were interrupted by Grandfather's voice. "Oh, Great Power," he called out in prayer. "We sit quietly in this sacred place following the ways handed down to us since the beginning. We are mindful of spirit all around us. As we take into our bodies the breath of life, we acknowledge that all things share the breath of life with us—the rocks, the plants, the animals, the earth herself. We breathe our awareness that the earth is alive and conscious—one living whole of which we are a part."

Running Antelope, his eyes still closed, listened intently to Grandfather's words. He felt calmness come over him that he welcomed. When Grandfather stopped, he heard Burrow Ahead speak his prayer, as if his and Grandfather's were one. "And we acknowledge our obligation to respect life in every form—in our thoughts as well as our actions. We understand that a man should never wish harm to another man, for such thoughts sent through spirit would bring harm to both."

Dark Cloud Coming then continued the prayer, "We understand also, Great Power, that a group of people, such as those of us here, should never wish harm to another group of people, for such feelings through spirit can result in destruction for both groups."

There was silence when Dark Cloud Coming finished. *The next turn in the circle belongs to Two Snakes.* Running Antelope opened his eyes to look at the one who felt grief as he did. Two Snakes, his eyes closed and his face grim, said nothing.

Grandfather broke the silence by clearing his throat. As if that was a signal, the others opened their eyes and looked up. Uncle got to his feet long enough to add another cedar branch to the fire before Grandfather spoke again. "We meet together because of what has happened at Kawaioukuh." The others nodded their understanding. "Some of us have heard Two Snakes and Running Antelope tell of their experiences, but those were not occasions for questions." He looked up at Running Antelope, softness in his expression.

Then, returning his attention to the others, he said forcefully, "Now is the time to ask questions."

The war chief motioned with his hand. "I have questions," he said. Then, looking at Two Snakes, "How many were there? How many white-faces and how many large animals?"

Two Snakes returned the look, his face still grim and darkness around his eyes. He answered with bitterness in his tone, "The animals—like giant dogs—each with a white-face on its back numbered as many fingers as you and I have on our hands. That is what we faced!"

Grandfather looked up at Running Antelope. "Is that the number you saw, my grandson?"

"Yes, my grandfather—and there were others who stood on the ground—perhaps as many as ten."

The war chief spoke again. "Tell us about their weapons." He looked first at Two Snakes.

"The white-faces on the giant dogs each carried a long shaft of wood—longer than a spear. It appeared to be heavy, and the end that was leveled at our faces came to a point." Two Snakes spoke with less emotion, but his eyes were narrowed as if his hostility toward the Spaniards was simply coiled, ready to be released. "They also carried knives as long as your arm," he added. "I believe they use these when their enemy is too close for the wooden shaft to be used."

The war chief looked at Running Antelope. "What weapons did the men standing carry?"

"I remember that some carried bows shorter than ours, but of thicker wood. I did not see them used. Others carried big sticks on their shoulders. When my friends and I walked near the white-face camp, one of them pointed this weapon at us. It gave a sound like thunder and part of it flew over our heads. It was too fast and small to see."

"I saw the big stick weapon used," Two Snakes interrupted. "It was used like a club to kill the Kawaioukuh chief. It must be heavy—like being hit with a small tree." He paused and his eyes narrowed as bitterness returned. "I saw it used the way Running Antelope described, also. It thundered and smoked, and sent its killing part into my brother's chest! Then the same ugly white-face who killed Running Antelope's father stuck his long knife in my brother to be sure he was dead!"

Dark Cloud Coming placed his hand on Two Snakes' shoulder and gripped it firmly. No one spoke as the young man struggled with his emotions. Running Antelope struggled with his, as well. Grandfather again broke the silence, "Just one last question for now. What can either of you tell us about their leaders?"

"I know of only one," Two Snakes answered, as calmly as he could. "He wore a headpiece of gold, unlike the others. He talked with our chiefs with the help of the A:shiwi. He sent men into the kivas against our wishes! He could have prevented the killing!"

Grandfather spoke again softly, "And you, my grandson?"

"I saw one other who appeared to be a leader. He wore a long robe and had no weapon. He was protected by the other white-faces...and, my grandfather, he wore a cross of peace at his waist!"

Grandfather's sharp, clear eyes went wide in surprise. The other men exchanged looks of wonderment and murmured among themselves—except for Two Snakes who was bent forward, elbows on his knees, head in his hands. Grandfather spoke and the others quieted. "What we have heard gives us much to think and pray about. We thank you, Two Snakes and Running Antelope. You both may leave now and give yourselves rest. We can talk again."

The light of a nearly full moon guided Running Antelope back to his mother's dwelling. Sounds from inside told him that his family was asleep. Wearily, he climbed the outside ladder to his sleeping place on the roof. "Thank you, my mother," he whispered, "for setting out my sleeping pelts and a blanket." He stretched out on his back and gazed up at the black, star-studded sky. *Growing Reed and Standing Blossom! You see these same stars! I hope you are well! I miss you both!* Exhausted, he began drifting off to sleep. *I miss you, Standing Blossom.*

7

Running Antelope and his father had planted corn in Mother's fields when the Sun Watcher announced that the sun was right. This was many days before Sun Father reached his northernmost point in the sky. When summer did arrive, tiny shoots of new green corn were already growing in the yellow, sandy soil.

The seed corn had been planted deep in the ground where the soil is moist—as deep as the length of a man's forearm. With the help of planting sticks, Running Antelope and Father poked many kernels into each hole, enough to allow for pestering insects and determined crows. They covered the kernels first with the damp soil from the bottom of the hole, then the topsoil. Weeds were left undisturbed so the soil would hold together protecting the growing corn. The two would frequently loosen the soil using digging sticks, but only to a shallow extent. The topsoil, then, could absorb the occasional mid-summer rains without exposing the deeper soil to erosion.

When Running Antelope and Father left for Kawaioukuh, the new corn stood as high as a man's knees. Rain Walk had stayed behind to cultivate Mother's corn, as well as patches belonging to his own mother. Now, with Running Antelope's return, the responsibility for all of Mother's crops rested with him.

"I am going now, my mother!" Running Antelope called out, having gathered together his bow, a quiver of arrows, his rabbit stick, a prayer stick, a digging stick, and an empty drinking gourd. He was ready for another day of work.

"Be careful, my son!" his mother called back from inside the dwelling. "Remember to keep good thoughts!"

"I will see you when I come to the spring for water, my brother," he heard Large Eyes Watching say. Then she laughed, "If this baby will ever fill his stomach!"

46

"I will be there, too!" Rain Walk chimed in. "Whenever your sister and mother tell me I can go!" He laughed loudly.

Running Antelope had been following a routine each day since the morning after his return from Kawaioukuh. He awoke when the village crier announced the coming of dawn and walked with his family to the mesa's edge for prayer. When they returned home, he enjoyed their company over a simple meal, usually cornmeal mush and piki. When he was ready to leave for the fields, he would let Mother know, and then walk the length of five dwellings to the initial footpath steps that dropped almost vertically toward the desert floor. His first destination was the spring just beyond Mother's melons. He usually arrived there as Sun Father cleared the horizon.

"You are early, my aunt!" he said, greeting the wife of Close In The Antelopes. She was waiting to fill her water carrier from the main issue of water coming from the ground. Another woman was ahead of her.

"The water here flows less and less each day, Running Antelope. It takes longer to fill my jar. If I am not early, I must wait much of the morning while those before me fill theirs."

When the woman finished, Aunt took her place next to the running water. She dipped a gourd into the stream, filled it, and then poured the water into the carrier through its narrow neck. "You can use your strong arms to lift the jar to my back when it is full. That is the hardest thing for me to do by myself."

"Of course, my aunt! It will give me happiness to help you," Running Antelope assured her. "While you fill your jar, I will place another prayer stick in the spring and pray that the Cloud People bring rain." He held out his prayer stick for her to see. It was of willow, as long as from his palm to the tips of his fingers. Half of its length had been painted blue as the sky. The other half was brownish red, the color of earth. Tied to the blue end was a slender string made of cotton—about the same length as the stick. Tied to the other end of the string was a small, white down feather of an eagle.

"That should attract the Cloud People, Running Antelope!" Aunt exclaimed. "Did you make it?"

"No, my father made it—and the other three I have placed here. He would put one in the spring every four days, as I have been doing. He would remind me that the feather's power to carry our prayer would be gone after four days."

"Your father was a wise man—and a good man. He is missed by everyone in our village."

Running Antelope stuck the brown end of his prayer stick in the wet sand of the spring, then closed his eyes and prayed silently. When he was through, he looked at his aunt with a smile of satisfaction. "I can help you now with your water jar, my aunt." He lifted the heavy vessel and set it down in her blanket, which was on the ground prepared as a sling. One side of the jar was flat to fit her back. She would carry it there with the blanket-sling supported by her forehead.

"Thank you," Aunt said after he lifted the wrapped carrier to her back and the sling was in place. "I am ready to return to my home. May your day go well, Running Antelope."

"May your day go well, also, my aunt," he replied with a wave. As he looked toward the mesa, he saw that Large Eyes Watching and Rain Walk were nearing the desert floor. He waved at them, too, then filled his drinking gourd from the spring and headed out to the corn.

The cornstalks, now almost as high as Running Antelope's waist, were in patches according to color. The largest patch would produce yellow corn, with smaller patches for blue, red, and white corn. The stalks were positioned to grow four paces apart in rows that were also four paces apart. He intended to inspect each one for signs of worms, and loosen the surrounding soil with his digging stick. He looked at the turquoise sky to check on clouds moving slowly toward the mesa. They were white and fluffy, like cotton ready for harvest. *No rain*, he thought.

When he reached the patch of yellow corn, a song Father had taught him entered his thoughts. The two of them often sang it together when they worked side-by-side. He began to sing it softly now as he turned dry soil with his digging stick.

Oh, Corn Mother
Oh, Mother of Man
Thank you for your gifts
Young sprouts to boil and eat
Young stalks to roast in ashes
First ears for mush and piki
Stunted ears for soup to drink
Perfect ears to give to babies

Thank you for your gifts
Oh, Mother of Man
Oh, Corn Mother

When the song ended, Running Antelope stopped digging and looked up at the sky again. "Corn is the heart of our people! Never forget that, my son," he said aloud in the way Father would. "I will not forget, my father!" he answered himself. "I will not forget!"

ᚾ ᚾ ᚾ

It was hot by mid-morning. Running Antelope returned to the spring to drink and refill his gourd, and then headed back to the patches of corn. He quickened his pace when he saw a flock of crows gliding in for a landing among the cornstalks. "Ai, hee! Ai, hee!" he cried out, picking up a handful of small stones and throwing them at the birds. "You will feel my arrows if you come back!"

ᚾ ᚾ ᚾ

By mid-day, Running Antelope had completed less than half of his work. He had just thrown his rabbit stick at a gopher and missed when Rain Walk called to him. "Are you hungry? Your sister brought us food."

"I am hungry! Hungrier than the gophers and rats around here should be. My stick is digging out their holes when it should be digging around the corn."

"I have the same problem in my mother's fields," Rain Walk sighed. "We should work together. It usually takes two of us against one of them!" He laughed his loud laugh, and then said, "We must eat first to build up our strength." They both laughed loudly.

Farther out from the mesa, but not far from the corn patches, was a shallow wash in which clusters of cottonwood trees grew. Their shade offered relief from the mid-day heat, and attracted many of those working in the fields. A small stream provided water to drink as it meandered within the wash, its trickle now no wider than one long step. Running Antelope and Rain Walk chose to sit on a stretch of shaded sand where they could lean their backs against the side of the wash.

"Oh-ee-e! Corn cakes!" Running Antelope cheered when he unwrapped the cornhusks protecting his meal.

"And piki, too," Rain Walk said, placing another cornhusk package between them before standing up. "Do you need water to dip yours in?"

"Yes, thank you," Running Antelope responded, handing him his empty gourd.

As Rain Walk turned and started toward the stream, he noticed Two Snakes approaching the wash. "Two Snakes! Come sit with us!" he called out, raising a gourd and waving it.

Two Snakes returned the wave and headed in their direction. When he stepped down into the wash, he saw Running Antelope and greeted him with a nod. He breathed a sigh as he sat down next to him. "It is cool here, and this sand is soft to sit on. You have found the perfect place to rest."

Running Antelope finished a mouthful of corn cake before he spoke. "We usually find shade farther upstream, but all the good places are taken. Perhaps we will come here from now on. You can join us if you wish."

Rain Walk returned with the gourds of water. "Yes, join us anytime. The days are hotter now. It would be good to work early in the day and late in the day—and rest here while Sun Father is midway on his course. I could probably get more sleep here than I do at home!" he laughed loudly at himself.

"We need...to see rain...walking through our rows of corn," Two Snakes said haltingly as he chewed a bite of his own piki. "That would cool us off, too." He looked at Running Antelope. "There has been no rain since the day before we left for Kawaioukuh. It may require the help of our snake brothers for rain to come soon enough to save our corn."

"That is true," Rain Walk agreed. "Without our snake brothers, we could soon be eating the sand we sit on." He did not laugh this time.

Running Antelope nodded. "The summers I remember have been like this—not enough rain for our corn to reach full growth—until the Snake priests danced the snakes."

"Yes, and I have been one of the Snake priests," Two Snakes added, "and so has Rain Walk. And we will be Snake priests again soon." Rain Walk nodded in agreement as Two Snakes continued. "It is tonight that the crier will make the announcement—after the chiefs meet in the Antelope kiva to smoke and pray. He will tell our village that tomorrow at white dawn the ritual for dancing the snakes begins as the Sun Watcher has said it should."

Running Antelope shifted his place on the sand so he could sit cross-legged facing Two Snakes and Rain Walk. "My father was a Snake priest, too!" he said, enthusiastically, his eyes bright and eager, "and I am to be one!"

"I know that is true. Your father had a pure heart and our snake brothers knew he was their good friend." Two Snakes looked directly at Running

Antelope. "He would want you to be a good friend of our snake brothers, too. You are almost a man. Perhaps it is time for you to help us dance the snakes."

Running Antelope swallowed hard, his eyes wide and unblinking. "How would I learn to do that?" he asked, respectfully.

Two Snakes smiled. "My brother was your ceremonial father, but he is now with the Cloud People. Until a new ceremonial father is chosen for you, I can help you learn."

Running Antelope nodded his head slowly. "I know this is what my father would want—and Big Bull Snake, too." Looking first at Rain Walk, then at Two Snakes, he said firmly, "I would like that!"

ᴎ ᴎ ᴎ

Running Antelope and Rain Walk worked together the rest of the afternoon. They succeeded in ridding their corn patches of several gophers and rats, and brought down three rabbits with throwing sticks in the process. Sun Father was well into his descent when the two walked wearily toward the mesa. They waved at Two Snakes, who was still working in a patch of corn. Rain Walk spoke in a quiet voice, "Since Big Bull Snake is no longer here, Two Snakes has his mother's corn to look after, as well as the corn of his wife's mother."

"I have seen that he remains here working after most men have returned to the village," Running Antelope said just as quietly.

"Did you know that Two Snakes and I have the same number of summers?"

"No. How many do you have?"

"I have twenty summers. When we were young boys, he and I often played together. Now we are growing old together!" Rain Walk chuckled, looking at Running Antelope for a reaction.

"Grandfather has said that he gives no thought to such things," Running Antelope responded in a serious tone. "He tells us that there are many more important things to have in our thoughts. But...if you wish to think about growing old...I will cut for you a sturdy walking stick so you can keep up with me when we walk to the fields and back." They both laughed loudly and raced the rest of the way to the mesa's base.

8

The first day of the snake dance ceremonial period Two Snakes had spoken of was no different for Running Antelope than any other day spent in the fields, except for the excitement and anticipation he felt. These feelings were even stronger now as he waited by the Snake kiva where he was to meet Two Snakes. Sun Father was drawing close to his western kiva, and Two Snakes was nowhere to be seen.

Running Antelope, wearing only a breechcloth, stood outside a circle of cornmeal drawn on the powdery sand around the kiva. It reminded him of the line of cornmeal drawn in front of the white-faces at Kawaioukuh. *I am not to step across until I am invited.*

Something else was different at the kiva, too, Running Antelope noticed. Tied across the top of its ladder, well above the top rung, was a long hunting bow with large red-stained eagle feathers hanging from its bowstring. There was also the black and white pelt of a skunk tied above the top rung.

"The red feathers are the light and warmth we receive from Sun Father," Two Snakes commented as he approached Running Antelope from behind. He, too, wore only a breechcloth, except that in his loose, shoulder-length hair was a small red feather tied near the crown of his head. "Sun Father's light and warmth spread everywhere like the strong smell of a skunk. Anyone who looks up at the ladder can see that this kiva is taking part in ritual. The cornmeal at your feet warns those not taking part to stay away."

"I remember my father telling me these things," Running Antelope sighed, "but it seems so long ago."

"I have been in the Antelope kiva with the Antelope priests and my brother Snake priests. The pipe was lit and we let its smoke carry our prayers to the Cloud People as we will do each of the twenty days of ritual. My Snake brothers will be here soon. You and I can enter the kiva now and wait for them."

Running Antelope stepped up onto the kiva's roof and followed Two Snakes toward the ladder. He walked carefully when he came to a layer of sand that had been sprinkled on the roof around the entrance. Drawn on the sand with cornmeal were six lines radiating from the roof opening. Two Snakes paused at the ladder and spoke again. "The lines of cornmeal are the directions from which the Cloud People can bring us rain—north, east, south, west, above, and below."

Running Antelope nodded his understanding and followed Two Snakes down the ladder. As he reached the raised ledge that extended around the kiva's perimeter, he heard men talking above him and felt the ladder shaking. He moved out of the way as the Snake priests descended and continued on to the kiva's floor where they joined Two Snakes. Rain Walk was among them. Running Antelope sat down on the raised ledge to watch and wait.

There were twelve Snake priests, including Two Snakes and Rain Walk, each with a red feather worn high on the head and long hair worn loose to the shoulders or upper back. Their perspiring bodies glistened in the light of a coal and cedarwood fire. Conversations and occasional laughter filled the kiva with sounds as the priests squatted on the floor or sat on the raised ledge in twos and threes, busying themselves with the contents of several basket trays.

Two Snakes walked over to where Running Antelope was sitting. He held up a red-stained downy feather tied to a short piece of yucca thread. "This prayer feather is for you to wear," he said as he secured it to Running Antelope's hair. He stepped back and grunted his approval of its appearance before announcing, "We will make prayer sticks as the others are doing." He turned and motioned to Rain Walk who handed him a bundle of long, thin willow branches tied together with a strip of deerskin. He passed the bundle on to Running Antelope and was next handed a basket tray, empty except for a stone knife. He set the tray on the ledge and spoke again. "Use the knife to cut the branches in lengths as long as your longest finger. Tell me when the tray is filled with sticks." He started to turn away, then paused and looked back at Running Antelope. "Keep good thoughts as you work. Keep thoughts of rain and of ripened corn ready for harvest." He nodded his head for emphasis and then joined a group of priests sitting near the fire pit.

Running Antelope set the bundle of branches next to the tray and tested the knife gently against his finger. Satisfied with its sharpness, he pulled out a branch and held the thicker end against his open left hand. With his thumbnail, he marked a length comparable to his middle finger. He laid the stick on the stone ledge and carved at the nail mark with the knife. Soon the branch snapped in two, with one piece the desired length and ready for the basket tray. He repeated the process until the branch became too thin of a twig to use before pulling out another one from the bundle and treating it the same way. He worked steadily with only his thoughts to keep him company—thoughts of rain and ripened corn, of course—but thoughts also of his father who brought him to this same place to teach him ceremonial songs and dances, and to tell him stories about their people that he had been told by his father.

When the last branch had been cut and the basket tray was full, Running Antelope gathered the leftover twigs and piled them neatly beside the tray. He sat again on the ledge and waited until Two Snakes looked his way, then nodded his head to let him know that the task was finished.

Two Snakes returned carrying in one hand a pottery bowl filled with a thick, yellow liquid, and in the other hand, several pieces of arm-length cotton string. He set them on the ledge next to Running Antelope, and then took several willow sticks from the basket tray and tied them together with one of the strings. "Now you are to tie sticks like this," he instructed, "and put them in the bowl to soak. When they have taken in the yellow, pull them out with the string and tie them to the ladder above the fire pit to dry in the fire's smoke."

Running Antelope took the sticks he was handed and forced them into the dye with his fingers. When Two Snakes nodded, he pulled the sticks out, allowed drippings to return to the bowl, and then took them to the ladder and tied them to one of the rungs. He stepped back to watch the smoke envelop them as they swayed back-and-forth in the moving air. As he returned to his workplace, Two Snakes rejoined his brother priests.

И И И

The tenth bundle of sticks was the last one to hang from the ladder. Running Antelope gazed at them, happy that his work had gone well. As he looked, he noticed that a change in color had begun to take place in those sticks hanging the longest. His brow wrinkled in dismay and he called softly to Two Snakes, "The yellow is going away! Is this supposed to happen?"

Two Snakes glanced at the hanging sticks and nodded with a slight grin. "Yes. The sticks are turning to a reddish-brown, the color of the soil from which our corn grows. They will remain there in the warm smoke during the night. We can leave now. When we return tomorrow, they will be ready for prayer feathers."

54

The next evening, Running Antelope returned to the Snake kiva. This time, he crossed the cornmeal border on his own and again entered the sacred, ceremonial chamber as far as the elevated seating ledge. He knew not to go on to the floor level unless invited. He sat cross-legged on the ledge near the foot of the ladder to wait for the Snake priests' arrival. In the dim light from the ever-flickering fire, he noticed that the hanging bundles of sticks had been taken down and placed in basket trays next to the *sipápuni*. Memories of his father's teachings came to him as he fixed his eyes on this small, round hole in the floor just beyond the fire pit. In his mind, he could hear his father's voice explaining: *The sipápuni is the opening to the world below out of which our people came in the beginning. It is found near the salt caves along the Great Red River to the west. The Six-Point-Cloud-People emerge from there when they bring rain to our corn. A sipápuni in every kiva keeps these thoughts with us.*

Footsteps on the roof brought Running Antelope's attention to the opening above him as it filled with figures of Snake priests coming down the ladder. He stood exchanging nods of greeting with each one as they passed by him. Two Snakes was last. He nodded at the basket trays in the center of the floor. "We will finish these, then cut branches for more." He stepped down onto the floor and picked up two trays. One contained reddish-brown willow sticks; the other a pile of small, fluffy feathers and some slender lengths of cotton string. He handed both trays to Running Antelope. "The feathers of eagle breasts are as light as the Cloud People our prayers reach. You tie one to each stick. The string is cut to a stick's length." He sat down on the ledge and picked up a stick and a piece of string. "Hand me your knife," he said as Running Antelope sat down. Stretching the string alongside the stick, and then holding the cutting place with thumb and forefinger, he cut the string, carefully tying one end to a downy feather near its quill and the other end to one tip of the stick.

Running Antelope followed his example by picking up a stick and holding a piece of string against it. "This stick has been painted with raindrops," he said, noticing a series of small, black marks along its length.

Two Snakes nodded. "Some of my brothers were here while you and I were still with the corn. There is much to be done before we dance the snakes."

The two worked side-by-side until the last stick in the tray had its feather. Then, while Two Snakes mixed yellow dye from the flowers of the *hohoí si* plant, Running Antelope cut willow branches into finger-length segments. They stopped work for the evening when Sun Father was about to disappear into his kiva, and bundles of drying sticks were once again hanging from the ladder.

И И И

After four days of ritual activity, basket trays filled with prayer sticks crowded the kiva floor near the fire pit and the *sipápuni*. During the evening of the fifth day, Running Antelope helped with the making of snake whips. Two Snakes explained. "Whips are the prayer sticks we use when we hunt the snakes. If a snake is coiled, a whip is waved over it until it uncoils. Then it can be picked up." He handed Running Antelope a willow stick. It was as green as a cornstalk, with black dots painted on it from end-to-end.

"This is longer than the sticks I cut," observed Running Antelope. "Where is its prayer feather?"

"Yours is in your hair," Two Snakes replied, nodding at the small red feather near the crown of Running Antelope's head. "When we hunt the snakes, you will tie your feather to the whip you use. It will carry your prayers for a good hunt."

И И И

During the next few days, Running Antelope made more snake whips and lined them up against the raised ledge at the western end of the kiva. He also sang ceremonial songs with the Snake priests—prayerful songs about Sun Father and Corn Mother—about the Cloud People and rain—and about a rich harvest of colorful, mature corn.

When the priests danced, Running Antelope was invited to join them. He fell in line behind Two Snakes as the men circled the kiva floor, moving forward, swaying slightly to the left and to the right. The soft rattling of gourds and seashells helped him follow the swaying movements of the others. Each time he passed the *sipápuni*, he bent his body forward and stamped the dirt floor once with his right foot, as he saw the others do. When the priests began to sing softly, he joined in, the prayerful words coming easily to him now.

И И И

As the long period of ritual continued to unfold, Running Antelope spent late afternoons and evenings in the Antelope kiva. He sat quietly on the raised ledge watching the Antelope priests construct a simple altar in the middle of the kiva floor just beyond the *sipápuni*. The base of the altar was a sand picture as long and as wide as a man's leg. It was bordered by four bands of colored sand—yellow, blue, red, and white—separated from each other by black lines. At each of the four corners was a small cone of sand with a hawk feather stuck in it. Arranged on the enclosed field of white sand were colorful drawings of figures, shapes, and symbols that he did not fully understand. He gradually learned, however, as individual Antelope and Snake priests sat with him and spoke to him mouth-to-ear about ceremonial secrets.

By the evening of the ritual's eleventh day, the altar was almost finished. Running Antelope helped by going to the spring for water. He placed a prayer stick in damp sand before filling the large jar he had been given. When he returned, the priests poured the water into bowls that they placed on both sides of the altar's backdrop of cornstalks, prayer sticks, and buzzard feathers.

"Tomorrow we hunt the snakes," said Two Snakes as he sat down on the ledge. He looked at Running Antelope, a smile on his usually somber face. "Bring a digging stick with you. We will meet at the Snake kiva soon after Sun Father's face can be seen."

Running Antelope smiled in return. "I will be there," he replied confidently. "We will find many snake brothers who will let us dance them."

Two Snakes nodded, his face now serious. "Their spirits will take our prayers to the Cloud People and convince them to bring rain for our corn."

9

Sun Father had just cleared the eastern horizon when Running Antelope and Rain Walk arrived at the Snake kiva. Snake Moves Sideways greeted them cheerfully, as did other priests who were just arriving. Two Snakes stuck his head out of the kiva entrance and waved at them, and then climbed out onto the roof carrying bundles of snake whips under one arm. He smiled his greeting, stepped off the roof, and held the bundles in outstretched hands toward Snake Moves Sideways. The chief sprinkled the whips with cornmeal from one of several small deerskin bags that were sitting along the edge of the roof. He then motioned for each of the others to pick up a bag while Two Snakes distributed the whips.

Running Antelope reached up to untie the red feather in his hair as he saw the others doing. He then tied the feather to the end of the cotton string dangling from the snake whip he had been given. "I am ready!" he said firmly, catching the eye of Two Snakes. Two Snakes smiled his rare smile and nodded, and then looked over at Snake Moves Sideways. The chief was waving his arm in the direction of the footpath that had its beginning only a few paces from where they stood. Leading the way down the side of the mesa, he frequently turned toward those behind him to share in a laugh or make light conversation.

Two Snakes caught up with Running Antelope when they reached the base of the mesa. "You have your digging stick, a snake whip, and a bag of sacred cornmeal," he said softly, "but what is in your heart?" He paused before continuing. "Snakes do not fear us. They do not feel anger toward us. They will coil and strike at us only if our hearts are not right. They can see what is in our hearts." He paused again. "Keep a good heart!"

The group headed east to the spring to plant prayer sticks in the moist sand before turning north. They walked single-file along the edge of corn patches where the rough terrain supported wild grasses and desert plants. Dry cornstalks rattled in the morning breeze causing Running Antelope to gaze at them thoughtfully, knowing of their need for water. The words Two Snakes had spoken occurred to him. *Keep a good heart!* He repeated the words in his mind's voice as memories of his father entered his thinking. "Your heart was good, my father," he whispered. "My heart will be like yours."

The corn was behind them, but still in view, when the chief's sudden shout caused the line of priests to stop. Two Snakes turned toward Running Antelope and motioned for him to follow along to where the chief was standing. When they got there, the chief nodded at tracks in the sand. "Rattlesnake!" he said, smiling at Running Antelope. "It has gone after a mouse!" He nodded again, this time at a hole in the ground where the tracks came to an end. "Use your digging stick, but be careful not to hurt the snake. When you have uncovered it, pray in your heart for it and sprinkle it with sacred cornmeal. Then you can pick it up."

Running Antelope, his dark eyes shining with excitement, dropped to his hands and knees in front of the hole. With his head close to the ground, he peered into it. "I can see the end of the snake!" he said, his voice confident. Rising to his feet with digging stick in hand, he forced its blade into the ground at the side of where he knew the snake's tail to be, and then loosened the soil under and around it. Moving to his right a short step, he dug a second time the same way. "I can see the snake!" he said, sending his stick into the ground a third time. The priests cheered him on as each thrust of his digging stick exposed more of the large rattler.

"The snake has eaten the mouse," the chief observed, pointing to a bulge in the snake's midsection. "It is now too heavy to move quickly."

"You will see its head soon," Two Snakes added. "Your whip and bag of cornmeal are on the ground where you left them. Wave the whip over the snake if it begins to coil."

The rattler remained still as Running Antelope uncovered its head and sprinkled cornmeal over the length of its body. He again dropped to his hands and knees, his face close to the snake's head. "Brother snake," he said softly. "We need your help in bringing rain to our corn. Our fields are dry, and the stalks beat against themselves in despair." He arose to sprinkle another handful of cornmeal, then leaned over the snake again and continued in a whisper. "Brother snake, I ask that you come with me. I will be good to you and treat you with respect."

The snake began to move forward as Running Antelope reached for it. "Grab it behind its head," Two Snakes advised.

"I have it!" Running Antelope said, rising to his feet with both hands holding the twisting snake behind its head.

"Spit in the palm of one hand and stroke the length of its body. It will recognize the respect you have for it."

Running Antelope adjusted his grip on the snake and released his right hand. He spit in its palm and gently brushed the snake's body several times from the back of its head to its wriggling tail. Soon the long rattlesnake hung limply from his raised left hand.

Two Snakes walked up to him carrying a large sack made from a cotton blanket. "Put our snake brother in this," he said holding the sack open. Running Antelope dropped the snake into the sack and Two Snakes tied it closed with a strip of buckskin. "Be ready to open it for more of our brothers as we continue the hunt," he advised, handing Running Antelope the sack. "You get to carry them!"

И И И

By early afternoon, the priests had gathered ten more snakes, including three rattlers. The sack was heavy, and Running Antelope sighed with relief when the chief announced, "The hunt is going well! We can return to our homes now for food and rest. Tomorrow, we hunt to the west of our village."

Running Antelope and Two Snakes walked together as the group headed back. Two Snakes pointed at the tall mesa. "Tomorrow, we hunt on the other side. The day after, we go to the south. On the last morning, we return here and hunt to the east. Soon after, we will dance our snake brothers and the rain will come."

И И И

The final day of snake gathering began with a race soon after daybreak. Running Antelope had spent the night in the Snake kiva witnessing sacred ceremonies, and singing and dancing with the priests. He also painted his body a dark brown for the upcoming race, as the others did. They all left the kiva before dawn and descended the footpath to the desert floor by moonlight.

"You can run with us," Two Snakes said, motioning for Running Antelope to accompany him, Rain Walk, and two other priests. "We will go to the starting place while the others stay here to gather vines and cornstalks." The five started off at a brisk walk along the familiar route toward the southeast. Running Antelope's thoughts turned briefly to the events at Kawaioukuh before focusing on Two Snakes as he broke into a fast jog across the rough terrain.

The five runners did not stop until they reached the base of Huckyatwi, the isolated butte that looked like a huge badger rising abruptly from the desert floor. They were soon joined by a similar group of Antelope priests, each painted ash-gray from head-to-toe. After an exchange of greetings, one of the Antelope priests drew a cornmeal line along the ground in the direction of the village, and then waved his empty cornmeal sack in the light of early dawn. The race began.

They ran together the first half of the race, joking and laughing, with one of the Antelope priests setting a fast, but comfortable pace. Beads of sweat on brown and gray backs were glistening in Sun Father's rays when they caught up with an older Antelope priest jogging along ahead of them. Like the racers, he wore only a breechcloth, his long, black hair loose and flowing. He carried a gourd of water in one hand and several prayer sticks in the other. The leading Antelope racer increased his speed to insure that he would be the first to reach the older priest, and was handed the gourd and prayer sticks. The older man shouted to him, "Thank you, my brother! Carry those to our village! May Sun Father and Corn Mother bring gifts to our people!"

Running Antelope and the other racers kept the pressure on the lead runner who frequently looked back to see if anyone was gaining on him. Patches of corn were in view when another Antelope priest burst forward to challenge the leader. As the two ran side-by-side, the leader handed over the gourd and prayer sticks to his challenger, shouting, "Take these to our village, my brother! May Sun Father and Corn Mother bring gifts to our people!"

As the runners raced by the corn patches, the priests who had remained there urged them on, yelling and waving green cornstalks and vines of squash, beans, and melons. Some whirled thinly cut sticks on strings producing a sound similar to the rumbling of thunder.

The racers slowed as they reached the incline at the mesa's base, but continued to press the new leader as they scrambled up the steep trail. All of the priests from below followed them up to the village where cheering crowds lined the mesa's edge or stood on rooftops. When those carrying cornstalks and vines arrived in the center of houses and kivas, happy villagers rushed over to tear off pieces to take home.

Running Antelope enjoyed the laughter and excitement of his people as he sat resting on the edge of the Snake kiva's roof. Two Snakes sat beside him and nodded toward the nearby Antelope kiva. "Look." The race's winner had just come out of the kiva opening still carrying the gourd and prayer sticks. Running Antelope watched the priest step off the roof and head for the footpath at the mesa's edge. "He takes the sacred water and the prayer sticks to his wife's corn," Two Snakes commented as the Antelope priest disappeared from view.

Running Antelope added, "And when his wife's corn receives rain from the Cloud People, so will your wife's corn—and my mother's corn. We are all winners of the race."

И И И

Running Antelope was tired and the sack of snakes was heavy when the final hunt ended shortly after midday. The hunters had stopped at the stream east of the corn patches to wash brown paint from their bodies. "I want to go to my mother's house and sleep!" he said to Rain Walk as the two stepped out of the streambed.

"The same with me. Just a short sleep before we return to the kiva. We must prepare ourselves for the Antelope dance—the dance that will encourage the Cloud People to fill the sky above our corn."

"But first, I must take our snake brothers to the kiva and put them in their jars," Running Antelope sighed. "And I must feed them corn pollen. Sleep will have to wait."

"I will help you, my brother. Then we both can rest."

10

The center of houses and kivas was a wide stretch of pathway on the east side of the mesa's narrow top where ceremonial dances were held. At its southern end was the Antelope kiva, which had been constructed closer to the houses than to the mesa's edge. The other four kivas— Snake, Badger, Flute, and Rain Cloud—had been dug only a long step away from the mesa's eastern edge, and formed the eastern boundary of the ceremonial space. The Rain Cloud kiva marked its northern end, and the row of houses up the center of the mesa was the western boundary. It was within this windswept expanse high above the desert floor that the Antelope dance—and then the Snake dance—would take place.

For the Antelope dance, a shallow hole had been dug between the Antelope and Snake kivas. It represented the *sipápuni*—the opening to the world below. Covering the hole was a cottonwood plank as wide as two hands. Just beyond the *sipápuni*, a low circular shelter had been constructed. It was framed with cottonwood boughs and filled in with leafy branches. Its entrance was covered with a cotton blanket. Inside, Antelope priests had placed several bundles of green cornstalks, each tied together with squash, bean, and melon vines.

As Sun Father approached his western kiva, the heat of the day gave way to a chilly evening. The men, women, and children of the village—many with blankets wrapped around them— crowded the rooftops and fronts of houses facing the center. Shouts of approval came from them when Antelope priests began to file out of their kiva. The priests were led by Close In The Antelopes who carried the hunting bow with red-stained eagle feathers that had been tied to the top of his kiva's ladder.

Added to the gray paint on the bodies of the priests were zigzag lines of white on chests, arms, and legs. On faces, lines of white extended from the corners of mouths to ears, and chins were painted black. Each wore a white cotton waistcloth decorated with rain cloud symbols in red and green. Also at the waist were fox-pelts hanging from behind and a deerskin bag of cornmeal on one side. Each wore a necklace of turquoise and seashells, and at the crown of the head, a small white feather. All but the chief carried a pair of gourd rattles.

Close In The Antelopes walked over to the Snake kiva and stepped up onto its roof while the twelve priests behind him formed a line nearby. He tossed sprinkles of cornmeal into the kiva's entrance before returning to the head of the line. Unhurriedly, he led the priests northward in front of the other kivas, shuffling his dusty feet to a rhythm kept by the shaking of rattles. Upon reaching the Rain Cloud kiva, he turned the procession around and led the priests slowly past the crowds in front of houses. At the *sipápuni*, he dropped a pinch of cornmeal on the plank and stamped his right foot on it vigorously. Each of the priests following him did the same in turn as he started them on another circuit of the center.

At the end of the fourth time around, the priests stopped near the cottonwood shelter and stood there continuing the shaking of their rattles. Running Antelope could hear them from inside the Snake kiva where he and the Snake priests waited at the foot of the ladder. "Are we going out soon?" he whispered eagerly to Rain Walk, his face beaming the excitement he was feeling.

Rain Walk smiled and nodded. "Now we are going!" he replied, turning to follow the other priests up the ladder.

The villagers again voiced their approval as the Snake priests filed out of their kiva. Snake Moves Sideways was in the lead carrying the decorated hunting bow from his kiva's ladder. The waistcloths of the priests were made of deerskin stained red and decorated with figures representing snakes. Body paint was limited to rough circles of white on arms and legs. Their long, loose-flowing hair was crowned with a single red feather, and each carried a snake whip and had a small bag of cornmeal tied at the waist. Running Antelope was at the end of the line behind Rain Walk.

The chief led the Snake priests around the ceremonial area four times. As they past the *sipápuni*, each of them dropped cornmeal on the plank and stamped it forcefully. Continuing to step to the rhythm of the Antelope rattles, they moved close to where the Antelope priests stood. The Antelope priests began to sing, their deep voices chanting with the shaking of the rattles. The

Snake priests pointed their whips toward the ground and bent their bodies forward, then backward while shifting their weight from one leg to the other.

As the singing and dancing continued, the priest next to Close In The Antelopes stepped over to the cottonwood shelter, lifted the edge of the blanket covering its opening, and pulled out one of the bundles of vine-wrapped cornstalks. Holding it in front of him with both hands, he turned to the others as a Snake priest approached him from behind and began to gently stroke his back with a snake whip. In this manner, the two strolled together back and forth between the two lines of swaying priests.

Running Antelope's thoughts were of clouds gathering in the sky as he moved with the rhythm of the rattles. He whispered the words the Antelope priests were singing—words about Great Power and the Cloud People—words about dark, moist clouds and their gentle rains that walk through rows of corn. He watched with half-opened eyes as the Antelope priest returned the cornstalk bundle to the shelter while another priest sprinkled it with water. The Antelope priests stopped singing. He sensed Rain Walk turning, so he turned and followed along as the Snake priests filed around the center four more times, shuffling their feet to the continuing sound of rattles.

Running Antelope was the last to enter the Snake kiva. Before descending the ladder, he glanced back at the ceremonial center. In the dim light of dusk, he could see the Antelope priests beginning their final circuits. "The dance is ending," he said aloud. "The sky will soon fill with clouds."

И И И

Running Antelope spent the rest of the evening on the kiva's raised ledge. He ate food brought to the kiva by wives of the priests, and when the meal was over and the priests went to the Antelope kiva to smoke and pray, he was left alone. Sitting beneath the ladder, he could look up through the kiva's entrance at the night sky. A luminous band of stars stretched north and south across it...but no clouds. *The clouds will come,* he said in his thoughts. His eyes shifted to the four large, clay jars that stood on the far side of the kiva's lower floor. Each had its circular opening covered with deerskin that had been stretched, vented with slits, and tied down. *Our snake brothers will deliver our prayers to the Cloud People,* he added with conviction, *and they will bring rain to our corn.*

И И И

"Wake up, my brother!" Rain Walk said with a laugh. "We have to get the sand ready!"

Running Antelope opened his eyes to see his sister's husband descending the ladder with a full blanket-sack over his shoulder. Two more priests followed, each with a similar load. The three carried the sacks to the center of the floor and set them down.

"Our snake brothers did not keep you awake with their whispering, I see," Rain Walk said with another laugh.

Running Antelope yawned, then stood up and stretched. "Are you saying that my ears are so big that I can hear snakes whisper?"

Rain Walk chuckled. "Help me prepare the sand so our brothers will have only good things to whisper about." He emptied each of the sacks on the hard dirt floor. "We will spread the sand to make a large circle," he explained as Running Antelope joined him, "then make it smooth with our hands so that tracks will be easily seen."

They both got down on their knees and went to work while the other two priests stirred up the coals in the fire pit and added cedar logs. "Thank you, my brothers!" Rain Walk called out as the fire flamed. "Now we can see what our hands are doing!"

Footsteps on the roof announced the arrival of the rest of the priests. Snake Moves Sideways was the first to enter. He smiled and nodded his greetings, then sat down at the edge of the sand. The other priests then sat down, cross-legged with knees touching, forming a circle around the sand. Rain Walk motioned for Running Antelope to sit on the raised ledge near the four clay jars.

Running Antelope watched intently as Two Snakes handed the chief a large, clay basin the size mothers use to wash children's hair. He placed the basin on the sand in front of him, then took out his bag of cornmeal and poured out enough to form six lines radiating from the basin— one for each of the directions from which the Cloud People can bring rain. A large gourd was then passed to him. He poured liquid from it into the basin six times. Before each pouring, he waved the gourd over one of the six directional lines. After the sixth pouring, he emptied the remaining liquid into the basin and dropped into it a small yucca root.

Two Snakes lit the ceremonial pipe and handed it to the chief. The chief smoked and exchanged formal greetings with those near him, and then passed the pipe to his right. When it came back to Two Snakes and he had his turn, it was put to one side and praying began. The chief was first, praying to Great Power in his deep, emotion-filled voice. Then other priests prayed aloud.

When the chief picked up a snake whip, the praying stopped and singing began—softly and in low voices—with each priest picking up a snake whip.

Rain Walk stood up and left the circle, motioning for Running Antelope to join him by one of the clay jars. "We will take off the cover and empty the snakes onto the floor," he whispered. "Then we will pick them up and hand them to priests sitting near the washing bowl." Running Antelope nodded, a confident look about him. Rain Walk untied the deerskin cover and removed it and then the two lifted the heavy jar and turned it over. A tangle of snakes fell out onto the floor. Rain Walk quickly grabbed one in each hand and passed them to a priest near the basin. Running Antelope did the same with a gopher snake and a racer. The priests placed the snakes into the basin of liquid, washed their heads, then released them onto the sand. "Get that one," Rain Walk said calmly, pointing to a rattlesnake slithering away from the others.

"I have it," Running Antelope replied, grabbing the snake behind the head with one hand. He spit in the palm of his other hand and stroked the rattler the full length of its body, then handed its limp form to a priest.

When the eleven snakes from the first day's hunt had been washed, Rain Walk and Running Antelope emptied the second jar of its wriggling contents, passing the snakes two-at-a-time to the waiting hands of priests. By the time they had finished with all four jars, almost fifty snakes were drying themselves on the sand.

Rain Walk again spoke quietly to Running Antelope, "If a snake crawls out of the circle, you are to pick it up and return it to the sand." Running Antelope spotted a bull snake doing just that and went after it while Rain Walk sat down again with the other priests.

The priests continued to sing to the snakes, their voices deep and calming. Running Antelope captured a runaway sidewinder and whispered to it soothingly, "Stay with us, brother snake. We want you to tell the Cloud People of our prayers. If they do not bring rain to our corn, our people will soon be without food." He then gently placed it back on the sand and stood back to watch. Several snakes were rolling in the sand. Others seemed to be gazing at the motionless men who surrounded them. One long rattlesnake slithered toward the chief. It stopped when it reached his crossed legs, lifted its head, and then crawled onto his lap where it rested. The chief's eyes were closed, and his expression remained peaceful—even kind, Running Antelope noted.

The singing continued until early dawn gave light to the kiva's entrance.

The priests slowly rose to their feet, one or two at a time, picked up a snake in each hand and returned them to the jars. They spoke quietly among themselves and came back to the sand for more snakes. Running Antelope quickly gathered the few that remained and then looked questioningly at Rain Walk. "Now we go down to the stream to bathe and wash our heads," Rain Walk said, smiling. "Then we race again!"

ਮ ਮ ਮ

Running Antelope was tired from lack of sleep, but he kept up with the pace set by Two Snakes. It was a fast pace, and most of the Antelope and Snake runners had fallen back. Earlier, after purifying themselves at the stream, the Snake runners had jogged out to Huckyatwi to join their Antelope brothers for the start of the ritual's last race. Now the runners were rapidly approaching the village where the race would end. A large crowd stood along the mesa's edge watching the runners far below them. Many were children wearing small ceremonial waistcloths and dabs of paint on arms and legs. Some carried cornstalks or young melons and squash.

"I am thinking that you want to be the first to reach the village!" Running Antelope called out teasingly. Two Snakes motioned with his hand for Running Antelope to pass him. Running Antelope laughed. "You are the strongest runner with legs longer than mine! I will stay where I am and watch you win!"

Two Snakes slowed enough to allow Running Antelope to catch up with him. "You run strong and fast like me, my brother!" he called out, breathing easily. "Someday you may run faster...but not today!" He bolted ahead with a burst of speed, the base of the mesa's steep footpath a few paces ahead of him.

"I will be happy just to finish this race!" Running Antelope called after him, as his own legs began the difficult climb.

When Two Snakes reached the top, both Close In The Antelopes and Snake Moves Sideways handed him prayer sticks. He then walked around the center of houses and kivas, breathing deeply and waving at villagers. Running Antelope and the other runners followed along, breathing heavily and greeting the crowds, as well. When they all reached the Snake and Antelope kivas, Two Snakes walked over to Running Antelope and placed one hand on his shoulder. "You are a strong runner," he said with sincerity. "While the priests smoke and pray in the Antelope kiva, you can go to your mother's house to rest." Running Antelope smiled at the idea. Two Snakes continued. "We will return to our kiva when Sun Father is midway on his course. Then we will prepare ourselves to dance our snake brothers." Running Antelope's smile grew even wider.

11

"Where are they taking our snake brothers?" Running Antelope asked as he watched Rain Walk and three other priests climb the kiva's ladder carrying bulging blanket-sacks over their shoulders.

"To the *kisi*," Two Snakes replied, referring to the shelter of boughs and branches used during the Antelope dance. "They will stay there until we dance." He stepped back to assess the dabs of white paint he was applying to Running Antelope's back. The paint had similarly been applied to Running Antelope's chest and forehead, and his face had been blackened. He wore a red-stained deerskin waistcloth with a fringe of antelope hoofs along its bottom edge. A small red feather was tied close to the crown of his head. "I am finished," Two Snakes announced, having stepped back for another look. "When I give you necklaces, a turtle-shell rattle to tie to your leg, and a snake whip, you will be ready."

"Thank you for helping me," Running Antelope said, his eyes bright with anticipation. "I will make sure that my thoughts are ready, too."

И И И

As Sun Father approached the mountains far to the west, the villagers crowded around the center of houses and kivas waiting patiently for the Snake dance to begin. They roared with excitement when the gray-painted Antelope priests filed out of their kiva with rattles shaking and began the first of four circuits around the area. When passing the *sipápuni*, each priest stamped his foot on the plank cover and dropped cornmeal on it. After the fourth circuit, they lined up near the *kisi* facing east and stood there swaying to the rhythm of their rattles.

The crowd cheered again when the Snake priests filed out of their kiva and began the four circuits. Running Antelope, at the end of the line of twelve, shuffled and swayed to the rhythm as never before. He felt a pleasant tingling sensation around the top of his head, and his feet seemed to hardly touch the ground. When he came to the *sipápuni*, he pictured in his mind the Cloud People in the world below ready to emerge with much-needed rain. He stamped his foot on the plank and called to them, "We are here, Cloud People! Please listen to our snake brothers when they tell you about our prayers!"

After the last circuit, the Snake priests formed their line to face the Antelope priests. As they all swayed to the rhythm of the rattles, the two chiefs began to sing. When the others joined in, Running Antelope closed his eyes and added his voice to the deep, throaty tones around him. It was a song he had sung many times in the kiva. It told of the Cloud People coming from all six directions to drop their rain on thirsty corn. It told of corn ripening to perfection in Sun Father's warmth—and of an abundant harvest that would *feed our families—feed our people.*

When the song ended, the Snake priests waved their whips in the air and formed groups of three. Running Antelope was with Two Snakes and Rain Walk, watching intently as the chief and his two partners approached the *kisi*. The priest who had remained inside with the sacks of snakes was holding a large rattler in his hands. The chief knelt down at the entrance, his whip tucked in the band of his waistcloth, and was handed the snake. He seized it with both hands and rose to his feet, the rattler's head pointing to his left. With eyes closed, he turned left and began to walk leisurely around the center. His first partner walked slightly behind him on his right, his left hand on the chief's left shoulder to guide him, and his right hand holding a snake whip. As they strolled along together, the partner stroked the chief's back with the whip. The second partner followed a few steps behind.

As the second and third groups received snakes at the *kisi*, the chief and his partners completed the one circuit and stopped near the line of Antelope priests. The chief placed the limp rattler on the ground and stepped back. His second partner walked over to the snake and waved his whip over it, then took a pinch of cornmeal from his deerskin bag. He said a loud prayer, threw the cornmeal in the direction of Sun Father, and then sprinkled a second pinch on the snake's head. Running Antelope continued to watch as the priest grabbed the rattlesnake at the back of the head and picked it up. He stood there holding it firmly as the chief and his first partner headed toward the *kisi* to receive another snake.

Two Snakes had just been handed a large bull snake. He moved off to his left to begin a slow-paced circuit with Rain Walk guiding him and rubbing his back with a whip. Running Antelope followed them, his eyes half-closed, his thoughts focused on rain. When their circuit was complete, Two Snakes laid the reptile on the ground and stepped back. Running Antelope walked up to the snake and gently waved his whip over it as it began to coil. "Brother bull snake," he said softly, "I ask that you be our messenger to the Cloud People. Please tell them that our corn must have rain soon if we are to have a harvest. Please tell them of the songs we sing and the prayers we speak." He reached for the bag of cornmeal at his side and took out a pinch of the coarse powder. "Thank you, Sun Father, for keeping us," he said, tossing the meal toward the west. "Thank you, brother bull snake, for helping us," he said, taking another pinch and sprinkling it on the snake's head. With his whip secure in the band of his waistcloth, he squatted down next to the bull snake and picked it up with both hands.

"Give our brother to one of the Antelope priests to hold," Two Snakes instructed him, "then you go to the *kisi.*"

Running Antelope walked over to the line of swaying priests and handed the bull snake to Thundering Hooves, the oldest son of his mother's sister. "Thank you, my clan brother," he said before stepping over to the *kisi.* As he squatted in front of its entrance, the priest inside handed him a big, yellow rattler. He grabbed its neck with his left hand and spit in his right palm before standing. Stroking the length of the snake, he closed his eyes and turned to begin his walk. Two Snakes guided him with a firm grip on his left shoulder.

The pleasant tingling sensation returned to the top of Running Antelope's head and spread throughout his body as Two Snakes stroked his back with a whip. He moved slowly and was hardly aware of the limp rattler in his hands. His mind easily focused on thoughts of rain, the Cloud People, and his father's spirit among them. *My father,* he said in his mind's voice, *I am walking in a dream...and you are here with me.*

"You can lay brother rattlesnake down right here," said Two Snakes. "Rain Walk will speak to it in prayer." Running Antelope opened his eyes and saw that they had returned to the line of Antelope priests. He gently placed the snake on the ground and stepped back out of Rain Walk's way.

The Snake priests had gone back to the *kisi* again and again until it was empty of snakes. Each Antelope and Snake priest now held at least two of the reptiles. They strolled about the ceremonial area raising them high for the villagers to see. Some of the women and girls in the crowd threw cornmeal at them. Running Antelope walked about with a lively young rattlesnake in one hand and a calm gopher snake in the other. The wide grin on his face told of the joy he felt over his role in the ceremony.

Snake Moves Sideways stepped away from the crowd having been handed a basket tray of cornmeal. Running Antelope watched him as he formed a large circle of meal on the ground about six paces across. Inside the circle, he drew six lines radiating from its center. When he finished and stepped back, the priests dashed up to the circle and lightly tossed their snakes into its center. Running Antelope threw his gopher snake first and then used both hands to toss in the twisting rattler. Several women and girls with basket trays approached the circle and threw handfuls of cornmeal upon the wriggling mass.

At a signal from Snake Moves Sideways, the Snake priests rushed into the circle, grabbed as many snakes as they could carry, and hurried down the footpath as fast as they could. Running Antelope wrapped a long gopher snake around his neck, seized the yellow rattler in one hand and a sidewinder in the other, and headed down the path with them. When they reached the desert floor, Snake Moves Sideways called out instructions. "Two Snakes, you go north. Rattles Shaking, east. Round Eyes Staring, south. My group will go around to the west. After you release our snake brothers, meet at the stream beyond the corn."

Running Antelope and Rain Walk followed Two Snakes northward in the dim light of dusk. The corn patches were still in view when they released the snakes. "Thank you, brother snake," said Running Antelope when he allowed the gopher snake to slip off his shoulders. "Thank you," he repeated as he let the rattler and sidewinder free near a cluster of boulders.

"I am hungry for sweet corn pudding!" said Rain Walk after releasing the snakes he had been carrying.

"I am hungry, too," said Running Antelope, "for sweet corn pudding and much more!"

"We can run to the stream," said Two Snakes, "and be the first to bathe and the first to return to our homes for food."

Running Antelope looked in the direction of the stream. "That will be easy," he said, taking a position behind Two Snakes as they started off. He lifted his gaze to see dark clouds passing further east. "The rain is coming," he said knowingly.

"Yes! The rain is coming."

И И И

It was late that night when Running Antelope climbed the ladder to his sleeping place. He and Rain Walk had just returned home from the kiva where they had gone after their meal. The final four days of ritual had begun during the night, and now it was time to rest before another day of work fighting pests in the patches of stunted corn. He stretched out on the sleeping pelts and drew a blanket to his chin. The sky above him abounded with stars, but he could turn his head and see shadowy clouds off toward the west and east. He closed his eyes to pray one more time, but sleep came upon him before he could begin.

Running Antelope dreamed. In his dream, he could feel rain wetting his face. He wanted to open his mouth to drink in the drops...and when he did, he awoke to find them real. It was raining. He sat up quickly and tossed his blanket to one side. Leaning over the edge of the roof, he called to his family, "The Cloud People are here! They have brought us rain!"

Rain Walk rushed out of the room, his arms outstretched as if welcoming a friend and his smiling face turned skyward to delight in the drops. Mother and Large Eyes Watching came out, too, only to hurry back in when the rainfall increased to a drizzle. Shouts and cheers spread throughout the village. Rain Walk added his voice in a burst of gratitude. "Thank you, Cloud People! Thank you, Great Power!" He scurried up the ladder to join Running Antelope. The two stood in the shelter of the food storage room talking and laughing, and watched the downpour. They remained there as the rainfall tapered off and the Cloud People slowly drifted to the south. They climbed down the ladder when the crier announced the coming of dawn, his resonant voice calling out from a rooftop near the center of houses and kivas. Large Eyes Watching, the baby, and Mother joined them, and they walked together along the wet, sandy pathway to the mesa's edge where the entire village would soon greet Sun Father.

И И И

During the remaining days of summer, the Cloud People brought more brief thundershowers. The gold-green cornstalks grew taller and sturdier, and the protected ears, though small, developed fully.

"I am told that tomorrow is to be the beginning of harvest," Rain Walk remarked as he and Running Antelope approached the corn patches for another day's work. "The crier will make this known to everyone today."

"The corn is ready!" Running Antelope agreed. "I will be happy to see ears of many colors hanging inside houses and drying on rooftops."

Rain Walk gave him an unbelieving stare. "But that means you and I will not be coming out here every day to play with the rats and gophers!" he said in mock seriousness. "And the worms and ants! And the crows!"

Running Antelope laughed. "That will make me even happier!"

"I will be the happiest! The first day of harvest is for families. Everyone will come out to gather the corn. My wife will help me...our first harvest together. Our baby can lie on his blanket and watch us. He can learn early!"

ℵ ℵ ℵ

As Sun Father disappeared into his western kiva, the crier sang a prayer song from a central rooftop—a song that announced the beginning of harvest season, and thanked the Cloud People, Sun Father, and Great Power for their gifts. Running Antelope listened with his family, added his own prayer in a whisper, then went with Rain Walk to the Snake kiva for more singing and praying.

Later that night, sleep came easily for Running Antelope in the comfort of his pelts and blanket. He was deep in a peaceful slumber when the insistent voice of Two Snakes roused him. "Wake up, my brother! Wake up! You must come with us!"

He opened his eyes and sat up, trying to remember where he had put his bow and quiver of arrows. "Have Old Enemies come to steal out corn?" he asked sleepily.

"Come with us. You can answer that question yourself."

"It is still night!" Running Antelope grumbled as he descended the ladder.

Rain Walk was waiting with Two Snakes. "I do not know what is happening either," he said with a shrug.

"Come with me and you both will find out." Two Snakes turned and headed toward the center of houses and kivas. As the three past the Antelope kiva, Running Antelope noticed several men standing quietly in the darkness beyond the Snake kiva. Grandfather and the clan chiefs were among them. When they spoke to each other, it was in whispers.

Two Snakes put his hand on Running Antelope's shoulder and steered him to the mesa's edge. "Look toward the spring and listen," he said in a commanding tone. "Tell me what you see and hear."

Running Antelope stared into the darkness. The stars and the crescent moon hid behind a thin layer of clouds offering little light. He heard the animal sounds before seeing the dark shapes that made them. "Giant dogs!"

he whispered with a gasp. He looked into the cold eyes of Two Snakes and swallowed hard. "The white-faces have come to our village!"

12

Flute Song Pleasing had been the village chief since long before his son's wife gave birth to Running Antelope. His leadership helped the Little People of Peace survive near-starvation when summer rains failed to come, and bloody clashes with Old Enemies when they came to steal. The arrival of the white-faces presented a threat just as serious. It showed in the burdened expression on the chief's face when the faint light of early dawn revealed the frightening intruders on the desert floor. He gazed in astonishment at the giant dogs standing among the strangely dressed men with hairy white faces. "We must find a way to make them leave," he uttered with a moan, his deep voice trembling with emotion.

Claw Feet stood with him assessing what they all were seeing. "I count ten and three of the animals and the same number of white-faces," the war chief said solemnly. "There are also two others that may be A:shiwi."

"Our arrows will not reach them from here," Close In The Antelopes said knowingly, "but we can stop them if they try to climb the path. Their animals would have to have wings!"

"And we have many large stones to drop on their heads," inserted Claw Feet.

Snake Moves Sideways joined the discussion by first clearing his throat loudly, then speaking forcefully. "If we are to make the white-faces leave, we must go down to where they are and attack them with every warrior we have!"

There was a long, silent pause as if the others were searching their minds for a response. Flute Song Pleasing motioned in the direction of the Flute kiva. "Let us continue to talk where we can light the pipe and allow its smoke to carry our prayers." Turning to Snake Moves Sideways, he said, "Two Snakes should join us...and Running Antelope, too."

Running Antelope entered the kiva last. He remained standing on the raised ledge near the ladder as the chiefs and Two Snakes formed a half-circle on the lower floor. He sat down when they seated themselves cross-legged facing the *sipápuni* and the fire pit. The seven men rested quietly in the dim light of flickering flames, their eyes fixed on the small round hole before them.

Close In The Antelopes picked up a ceremonial pipe, filled it with sacred tobacco, and lit it with a flaming stick from the fire. He passed it to Flute Song Pleasing who took several slow puffs. His lips formed words of prayer as he silently watched the smoke rise to the kiva's ceiling. With each passing, personal words of kinship were exchanged and prayers were softly spoken until the pipe was returned to Close In The Antelopes. Running Antelope watched his uncle take several puffs before setting it aside.

Flute Song Pleasing, his face strained with emotion, spoke out clearly in his low, rumbling voice. "Our people are safe here. The white-faces are too few in number to rush up the climbing path successfully. Our heavy stones would fall upon them and kill them. Their strange headpieces would not save them. But...our corn is waiting for us." He paused as his voice began to tremble. "Our corn is waiting for us," he repeated in a softer, controlled tone. "Our corn is our heart! We cannot allow the white-faces to keep it from us or destroy it!" He looked at the others and nodded, inviting them to speak.

Claw Feet cleared his throat first. "It would be good if they attack us. It would be good if they come up the climbing path to reach us. We would put an end to them quickly and go on with our harvest."

"How can we make them attack us?" asked Dark Cloud Coming, impatient and ready to argue.

Two Snakes turned his head to look at him. "We can invite them to come up here," he suggested quietly, his narrowed eyes cold and unblinking, "And when they are on the climbing path..."

"Is there not another way?" interrupted Flute Song Pleasing, his questioning eyes searching the faces of those around him. "Is there not a peaceful way?" His words were met with silence. "Our way is not to kill," he reminded the others, "for that would bring harm to our people! What else might we do?"

The stillness that followed the chief's words was broken by the sound of footsteps on the roof, and then the appearance of Rain Walk descending the ladder. He wore the waistcloth and cap of a warrior, and carried a knotted club in one hand. He stopped next to Running Antelope and spoke when Flute

Song Pleasing nodded to him. "One of the A:shiwi has started up the climbing path."

"Allow him to come," the chief responded. "We will meet with him where the path ends." He looked at the others. "Perhaps the answer to my question will come from the A:shiwi. Let us find out."

Running Antelope followed the men out of the kiva and walked behind them through the center of houses and kivas. Several warriors were waiting by the steps of the climbing path while others stood nearby alongside piles of large stones that were always at the ready. The A:shiwi was climbing the last few steps as the chiefs arrived to meet him.

Flute Song Pleasing signaled a greeting with his hands. The A:shiwi responded with his hands, then let out two sharp breaths through his mouth. "Hou! Hou! I speak some of your words." His voice was high in tone and heavily accented. "I speak to your people when they come to Hawikú to trade with my people."

Running Antelope stood with Rain Walk near the Snake kiva close enough to the chiefs to hear the A:shiwi. He stared curiously at the man speaking his greetings. He was small—shorter than Grandfather—and about as old. His straight, black hair had flecks of gray. His dark face was thin and wrinkled, but his dark eyes were clear and alert. He wore a decorated waist-cloth and vest of bison skins, and a necklace of seashells and turquoise.

Flute Song Pleasing returned the A:shiwi's breath greeting, "Hou! Hou!" Then he spoke in the A:shiwi's language, "I speak some of your words. I have traded in Hawikú many times."

Running Antelope, a look of surprise on his face, could only guess at the meaning of what his grandfather said. "I have never heard Grandfather speak like an A:shiwi!" he whispered to Rain Walk. Rain Walk nodded, but kept his attention on the A:shiwi.

The A:shiwi bowed slightly at Flute Song Pleasing and said in his own language, "I am pleased that you speak to me in the words of my people." Then, switching to the language of the men facing him, and using hand signs to supplement his words, he said, "The men I am with call themselves Spaniards. They and many others came to our village two new moons ago. Our warriors attacked them, but only wounded a few and killed some of their animals. They beat us back with weapons we have never seen before. Many of our warriors were killed. Now we stay alive by doing what they tell us. I have even learned some of their words to please them."

Flute Song Pleasing nodded his understanding and stepped over to the mesa's edge. His gaze followed its almost-vertical wall down to its rocky base, then over to the Spaniards standing casually in a group, some with eyes looking up in his direction. "Why have they come here?" he asked abruptly, turning toward the A:shiwi. "What do they want?"

"They want someone to show them the way to the Great Red River." The A:shiwi stepped to the mesa's edge next to the chief and pointed toward the west. "They have heard that your people know the way. That is why they are here."

If Flute Song Pleasing was surprised by the A:shiwi's words, he didn't show it. Instead, he turned and looked at the clan chiefs with his eyebrows raised and a slight grin on his face. They shifted their feet and smiled nervously in return. "Which of you will guide the white-faces to the Great Red River?" he asked them, his grin now gone.

The chiefs looked at each other, then back at Flute Song Pleasing, but none replied. Finally, Claw Feet spoke out grimly. "The white-faces are not to be trusted!" he warned. "Two Snakes has told us of Kawaioukuh and the A:shiwi tells us of Hawikú. The white-faces only want to trick us and kill us!"

"Claw Feet speaks the truth!" Two Snakes called out from behind the chiefs. "We cannot believe what the white-faces say! We should tell them that the Great Red River can be found without our help...by walking in the direction of Sun Father's path...and that they should leave now!"

"Perhaps you both are right," Flute Song Pleasing said calmly, nodding to the two. "But first, I want to meet the chief of the white-faces. I want to see his eyes and hear his voice." Turning to the A:shiwi, he said, "Let us go down the path to meet with the white-face chief. I can then decide what to do." Looking again at Claw Feet and Two Snakes, he said, "Both of you come, too."

Running Antelope moved closer to the mesa's edge and watched his grandfather lead the way. He could see the white-faces looking up at the four men stepping carefully down the steep, twisting path. Some were eating small, ripening melons that grew among tangled vines near where they stood. As grandfather's group reached the base of the mesa, three of the Spaniards left the melon patch and walked toward them. Pointing at the three, Running Antelope said, "The two who cover their heads with bright yellow caps are the chiefs."

"The other wears a cap the color of a gray wolf, "Rain Walk noted. "So do the ones eating our melons. Perhaps they are warriors like me."

"Their chiefs are talking with grandfather and the A:shiwi. They all use their hands as well as their voices. I would like to be there to listen!"

"I would, too. Look at Two Snakes. He just said something close to our chief's ear. Now he has moved away to stand by himself!"

"He has much anger toward the white-faces. He will never forget Kawaioukuh...and neither will I."

The two sat down on the low roof of the Snake kiva and continued to watch the scene below. Running Antelope's gaze wandered out to the spring where the animals were standing quietly, occasionally drinking water. "The giant dogs cannot be so dangerous if one A:shiwi can watch over them," he remarked. "He even pulls them by cords fastened to their heads to make them follow him."

Rain Walk grunted his agreement, then said, "Our chief has finished. He walks toward the climbing path with Claw Feet and Two Snakes."

"The A:shiwi is staying with the white-face chiefs. Perhaps they will leave now."

When Flute Song Pleasing reached the mesa top, he motioned to the clan chiefs to follow him and headed once again to the Flute kiva. As Two Snakes passed by, he caught Running Antelope's eye with a stern glance and signaled with a jerk of his head for him to come along.

The chiefs and Two Snakes took their places in the half-circle and sat quietly, their eyes closed. Running Antelope sat on the ledge and closed his eyes as he heard his grandfather begin to pray. "Oh, Great Power, we call to you from this sacred place with troubled hearts," Flute Song Pleasing spoke out clearly. "We wish no harm to anyone, yet danger has come to our village—strange men with weapons and animals that frighten our people."

Running Antelope nodded. *I have not been alone in my fear*, he said in his thoughts. *Everyone is afraid...except Grandfather!*

"Oh, Great Power," the chief continued. "We respect the life of every man. We do not want to take lives. If we refuse the demands of the white-face chief, we will risk his anger. If we attack the white-faces, we will risk even more." He paused, and then in a lighter tone said, "Thank you, Great Power! You have found us a better way to answer the white-faces—a peaceful way that will see them leave our village."

The astonished clan chiefs opened their eyes and stared at their leader, hardly believing what they had just heard. Running Antelope blinked open his eyes and leaned forward to catch every word yet to come. Flute Song Pleasing opened his eyes and looked at the others, a slight smile tugging at the corners of his mouth. "Two Snakes has told me that his thinking has changed. He will lead the white-faces to the Great Red River. We can soon return to our corn."

The clan chiefs exploded in cheers and jumped to their feet. They grinned and nodded at Two Snakes, and talked excitedly among themselves. Close In The Antelopes sighed in relief, resting a congratulatory hand on Flute Song Pleasing's shoulder. Snake Moves Sideways, who was next to Two Snakes, looked at his clan brother with raised eyebrows, then smiled and nodded his appreciation.

Running Antelope became aware of deepening admiration for Two Snakes. *This is what my father would do*, he thought to himself. *He would do this for our village—for our people. Two Snakes is brave like my father.*

As the voices of the chiefs quieted and they sat back down, Two Snakes stood up and raised his arm for attention. "I wish to speak!" he said loudly. "I want someone to go with me to the Great Red River!"

Talking abruptly stopped and smiles disappeared as everyone stared apprehensively at Two Snakes. Eyes shifted to Flute Song Pleasing whose expression of bewilderment was rapidly turning to anger. Before he could express himself, Two Snakes spoke again, softly this time. "I want Running Antelope to come with me."

Flute Song Pleasing glared at Two Snakes, his brow deeply wrinkled and his face a burning red. "Why did you not tell me this before?" he thundered. "Running Antelope is not yet a man! Why do you want him to go with you?" His voice trembled as his anger mounted. "Why not someone like yourself? Why not a warrior or clan brother?" He turned to look at Running Antelope who sat stiffly on the raised ledge, stunned by the words of both men. "Why my grandson?" he asked again, his voice taking on a softer tone.

Two Snakes, having waited calmly for the opportunity to respond, spoke out again. "Running Antelope knows the white-faces as well as I do. He knows of their weapons and their ways. He knows to expect their treachery. Together, we will not be fooled by them."

"He has never seen the Great Red River!" Flute Song Pleasing countered. "He has never journeyed that far! He is still a boy!"

"Your grandson is strong like his father. He is fast and untiring. He has journeyed to the Little River That Joins The Great Red River and to the Mountains of the Katsinam."

"Others have done the same and much more!"

Two Snakes studied his chief's face and saw anguish in his eyes. His response was respectful, but firm, "Since Kawaioukuh, I have taken my brother's place as Running Antelope's ceremonial father. Unless Running Antelope chooses someone else, I will continue to do that. There is much he can learn by coming with me to guide the white-faces—more than he would learn on a journey for salt or trade. He will be a man when we return."

Flute Song Pleasing looked at Running Antelope again, a distressed expression still on his face. "Come down here with us, my grandson," he said softly. Running Antelope did as he was told, his heart pounding like a ceremonial drum. He stopped next to the *sipápuni* and faced the half-circle of men he most respected. "My grandson," the chief continued, his voice once again forceful, "you have heard me speak of the danger that threatens our people, and of the peaceful way to remove the danger that Two Snakes offers. You have also heard him tell us why he wants you to join him in taking the white-faces to the Great Red River. I want you to speak now. Tell me what is in your heart."

Running Antelope looked to his right at Two Snakes, then straight ahead at his grandfather. Both men wore solemn expressions on their faces. Both waited in silence for his reply. "Two Snakes is my ceremonial father," his voice cracked with emotion. "He is my friend, as well. If he is willing to help our people in this way, then so am I. I will go with him to the Great Red River."

13

Don García López de Cárdenas, Captain of Cavalry, perspired profusely under his long- sleeved woolen shirt and steel vest. He cursed the heat of the midday sun, and then cursed the uncivilized natives who were keeping him waiting. "And these melons are green and tasteless!" he complained, throwing a rind to the ground.

"We will hope they get sweeter as they ripen," remarked Captain Megosa, his second-in-command. "Our men have picked many to take with us."

Cárdenas grunted his skepticism. "You had better tell them to take more corn and squash and fewer melons! We don't know how..."

"They are returning, my captains!" interrupted a cavalryman standing a few steps away. He was looking toward the top of the mesa, both hands shielding his eyes from the bright sunlight. "I see four of them."

The two young officers gazed upward to see for themselves. Cárdenas then removed his helmet, wiped sweat from his forehead with a stained sleeve, and spoke sharply to the cavalryman, "Galeras! Get the old man over here! It is time to force the issue with these simple-minded people and leave this miserable place!"

Running Antelope was close behind Two Snakes as they descended the twisting steps of the path. He glanced occasionally at the white-faces and saw that some were in the patches of corn. "They are taking corn!" he called ahead.

A grunt of acknowledgement was the only response he received until he came alongside Two Snakes where the path broadened before ending at the desert floor. "We can expect the white-faces to take what they want—like Old Enemies. They are men whose ways are evil."

The two caught up with Flute Song Pleasing and Claw Feet, and walked with them to where the three Spaniards and the old A:shiwi were waiting.

One of the gold-helmeted Spaniards was speaking loudly and angrily to the old man. The other two stood silently several paces behind them. Running Antelope whispered, "The one who is talking to the A:shiwi must be their chief like Grandfather is our chief." He looked at Two Snakes who gave him a slight nod.

Flute Song Pleasing signaled a greeting with his hand. The A:Shiwi responded in the same way, then spoke. "Hou! hou!" he began, with two quick breaths from his mouth. With hand signs and words, he continued, "The chief of the Spaniards wants to know if you have the guides he asked for. He wants to leave soon for the Great Red River."

Flute Song Pleasing nodded at the A:shiwi, then at Cárdenas. He cleared his throat and spoke in his deep, rumbling voice. "It pleases me to help the Spaniards by sending my own grandson and my sister's youngest son to guide them." He turned to nod at Running Antelope and Two Snakes, and allowed the A:shiwi to translate his words to the Spaniard. Looking at Cárdenas expectantly, he spoke again, "It is my prayer that Running Antelope and Two Snakes return safely to me when they are no longer needed."

Cárdenas gave no acknowledgement of the chief's words. His dark, piercing eyes sent a flickering glance at Running Antelope and Two Snakes and then returned to focus on Flute Song Pleasing. Though short and slender himself, he was taller than the native chief he faced by almost a head. He stood tall in his boots and looked down at the chief, "Are they ready to leave now?" he asked directly, in a tone of impatience.

When these words were translated by the A:shiwi, Flute Song Pleasing answered as though there was simply a matter of customary procedure to be followed. "We must prepare them for their journey. Prayers are to be spoken and the pipe is to be smoked. They must be with us in the kiva until the next yellow dawn."

Cárdenas frowned when the answer was explained to him. "Very well," he said gruffly, "We leave in the morning." As an afterthought, he turned and snapped, "Galeras! The trinkets!" Facing Flute Song Pleasing again, he made an effort to smile. "We have gifts for you."

The cavalryman Galeras stepped forward from behind his captain and held out two small cloth bags, each tied with a strip of the same gray woolen material. Cárdenas accepted the bags, untied one and took out a handful of lustrous white pearls to show the chief. After returning them to the bag, he opened the second one and pulled out a handful of small, ball-shaped silver bells. He shook them gently, opened his hand to show them off, and then returned them to the bag. Finally he handed both bags to Flute Song Pleasing.

Running Antelope hardly noticed the gifts. His eyes were on the white-face called Galeras—particularly the disfiguring scar that extended from his right cheek to the left side of his forehead. "That white-face!" he whispered to Two Snakes "He was at Kawaioukuh! Growing Reed and I saw him!"

Two Snakes turned, his body already stiffened and his fists tightly clenched. A flush of anger covered his face, and his cold, narrowed eyes briefly fixed themselves on Running Antelope's anxious eyes. He nodded once, but said nothing.

И И И

The entire village turned out for the departure of Running Antelope and Two Snakes. Friends and neighbors gathered where the footpath began its descent, some lining the mesa's edge, others sitting or standing on roofs of nearby homes and kivas. Relatives stood close by, showering the two with embraces and encouragement.

Flute Song Pleasing was the last to say good-bye. He held Running Antelope's shoulders in his large hands and looked deep into his eyes. "Your father's spirit sees you as a man and is pleased," he said proudly, "and so am I." Then, gripping the arms of Two Snakes, he said, "It is good what you are doing for our people. Your brother's spirit is pleased with you, as I am."

Running Antelope followed Two Snakes down the initial steps of the path. He had not felt so much emotion since leaving Standing Blossom and Growing Reed at Kawaioukuh. The burning lump in his throat was the same, as was the watering of his eyes. He shook his head to help clear his thoughts, and focused on each step he was taking down this steep and hazardous part of the path. The risk of falling was higher because of the load he carried. In addition to the bow and quiver of arrows hanging from a shoulder strap, the water gourd and pouch of sacred cornmeal tied to his waist, and the rabbit stick held in one hand, he carried a blanket-sack over one shoulder containing piki, small bags of cornmeal, extra gourds, a rabbitskin vest, a bowl for cooking and eating, an obsidian knife, pieces of flint, and prayer sticks. Two Snakes carried a similar load.

"The white-faces are out by the stream," Running Antelope observed.

"We will fill our gourds at the spring before joining them," responded Two Snakes, his tone somber.

The Spaniards had found shade under cottonwood trees growing in the shallow wash beyond the corn patches. There was adequate water in the stream meandering through the wash, so they had remained there overnight. Now they were breaking camp, saddling horses, and packing saddlebags as Running Antelope and Two Snakes approached.

"Over there!" yelled Galeras, who had stepped out of the wash and was watching them. "Get over there with the old man!"

Running Antelope didn't understand the words, but he saw the white-face-with-the-scar pointing at the A:shiwi standing near the white-face chief and his towering, coal-back giant dog. Two Snakes had already turned in their direction.

"It is about time you two got here!" Galeras yelled again. "Do not ever keep the captain waiting!"

Running Antelope ignored the anger in the man's voice and the words that had no meaning to him. He was staring in awe at the huge black beast he was approaching. It seemed to get bigger and bigger as he got closer to it. Out of the corner of his eye, he caught sight of something even more awesome. He stopped and called excitedly to Two Snakes. "Look! An A:shiwi is on the back of a giant dog!" They both stared in fascination as a young A:shiwi rode past them on a lively, reddish- brown horse pulling two other horses roped behind him. He proceeded to deliver the three animals to a group of waiting cavalrymen.

"These giant dogs might be harmless!" said Two Snakes, a look of surprise on his face. "That A:shiwi boy is not afraid!"

Running Antelope gazed in admiration at the boy who was now assisting cavalrymen with saddle blankets and bridles. "I have lived as many summers as he has, yet he rides the back of a giant dog and I am afraid to stand near one!" He shook his head in wonderment, then walked on with Two Snakes to where the older A:shiwi stood. The old man greeted them with a friendly smile and words they understood.

Captain Cárdenas looked them over silently, his bearded face set in a frown. "Neither one of them appears old enough to have been anywhere beyond this stream," he muttered. "Ask them if they have actually seen this great river we are going to."

The A:shiwi translated the question and Two Snakes responded. "I have been to the Great Red River," he said importantly. "I have lived with the Havasupai whose village is near its waters. Running Antelope has seen the Little River That Joins The Great Red River. That is where we will guide you first. We will then follow its waters to the Great Red River."

Cárdenas grunted his satisfaction with the reply as it was explained by the A:shiwi. Leading his stallion by its reins, he strode briskly away. "We will leave soon!" he called back over his shoulder, ignoring the A:shiwi boy who addressed him in Spanish as the two passed by each other.

The boy signed a hand greeting to Running Antelope and Two Snakes as he walked up to them. A wide grin exposed straight, white teeth that were a striking contrast to the dark brown skin of his face and the shiny, black hair that hung loosely down to his shoulders. He was as tall as Running Antelope, with a similarly trim waist and muscular upper body. Barefooted, he wore only a waistcloth of bison skin. "Hou! hou!" the breath greeting came from his mouth. "I am called Blue Stone Shining. Gray Fox Comes Out is my uncle," he said, nodding to the old A:shiwi. "We trade with your people when they come to Hawikú. We learn to speak like you!" He grinned again.

Running Antelope and Two Snakes greeted him in return and told him their names. Then Running Antelope asked curiously, "The giant dogs...they do not try to hurt you?"

Blue Stone Shining laughed loudly, his dark brown eyes laughing, too. "The Spaniards call them horses. They will not hurt you...unless you let them step on you!" He laughed again. "I was afraid until I learned to take care of them. Now I ride on their backs!"

Running Antelope's mind was racing, but Two Snakes interrupted his thoughts. "We are leaving now," he said, nodding at the Spaniards who had mounted their horses— and at Galeras who was riding their way, his long, sturdy lance pointing upward from its leather holder.

Gray Fox Comes Out nudged Two Snakes with his elbow and spoke in a low whisper, "That white-face...Galeras...has much hatred in his heart. It can be heard in his voice when he speaks to us."

Two Snakes looked into the eyes of the old man. "A heart full of hatred can bring death to a man," he whispered in return. "Let us go listen to what his heart has to tell us now."

14

Running Antelope quickly adapted to the fast pace set by Two Snakes. He was excited, and happy to be on the move. Taking his eyes off the landscape in front of him, he gazed up the vertical side of his mesa's southern tip, and then beyond to the blue sky filled with fleecy, white clouds. He uttered a prayer, "Oh, Great Power. Thank you for the Cloud People who pass over my village. Thank you for this journey I am taking to the Great Red River. I will learn much. My people will gather corn in peace. The white-faces will be happy."

It was not long before the mesa was behind them as Two Snakes led them in a southwesterly direction. "We are walking too fast!" cautioned Gray Fox Comes Out from behind Running Antelope. "The Spaniards are far behind us!"

Two Snakes stopped and turned to see for himself, a look of disgust on his face. "Little ants move faster than these white-faces," he snorted.

"Most of them walk with their horses," Blue Stone Shining pointed out, catching up with the three. "The horses carry much food taken from your harvest."

"Only the chiefs and the white-face-with-a-scar are on the backs of horses," observed Running Antelope when the riders topped a low, sandy ridge. He continued to watch as Galeras spurred his horse and charged in their direction.

"I told you brainless *moqui* that I will show you how fast to go!" Galeras hollered before pulling his horse to a stop in front of Two Snakes. "All you have to do is look at me!" he yelled again, stabbing at his chest with gloved fingers. "Tell him that, old man!" he barked at Gray Fox Comes Out before spurring his horse again and heading back to rejoin the officers.

Gray Fox Comes Out translated the essence of the message, knowing that "*moqui*" was a word the Spaniards were using to ridicule the native people. He looked at Two Snakes with understanding eyes when he saw the flush of anger on his face. "That white-face Galeras might hit you when you do something he does not like," he cautioned. "I know...and Blue Stone Shining knows," he added, soberly.

The expression on Two Snakes' face hardened, and he turned abruptly. "Let us go!" he said tersely, and strode off.

The travelers continued on toward the southwest at a much slower pace. The land was rough, with sandy mounds and ridges, grassy slopes, dry streambeds, and brush-choked gullies and ravines. Two Snakes followed a faint trail that Running Antelope could only occasionally detect. Tall mesas were off to their right, jutting southward from a high plateau. A vast, arid flatland was to their left, broken only by isolated rocky buttes towering over their surroundings.

Galeras frequently signaled for brief stops as loads required adjusting, or stones needed to be removed from horses' hoofs. He called for a much longer break when the sun was directly overhead, taking his orders from Captain Cárdenas. Horses were allowed to nibble on sparse grass as the Spaniards found shade wherever they could. They ate, and some tried to sleep.

Running Antelope and Blue Stone Shining found some shade under the branches of a treelike cholla cactus. They sat there sipping water from their gourds and eating piki. After swallowing his last bite, Running Antelope leaned toward his new friend. "Can you teach me how to ride on the back of a giant dog?" he asked, his eyebrows raised in anticipation.

Blue Stone Shining laughed loudly. "I had the same thoughts when my uncle took me to the Spaniards' camp near Hawikú. He told me that we were going on a journey with them, and that I was to take care of their big animals... feed them and find them water, and tie them together at night. I saw how the Spaniards rode on the backs of these animals, and how the animals obeyed them. I soon knew that I wanted to ride on their backs, too." He laughed again. "And you are just like me!"

They both laughed, then Running Antelope asked again, "Can you teach me?"

"I might be able to. I learned by myself when I thought no one was looking. I would lead a horse to stand beside a big rock. Then I would step up on the rock, grab the long hair on the horse's neck, and swing myself onto its back. I kept low...almost lying down...and let the horse take a few steps. Then

I would slide off and pretend to be feeding it. I did this many times before the Spaniards saw me."

"When they did see you, what happened?"

"Nothing! They watched me and talked among themselves, but did not tell me to stop. So I rode more! Then, before we arrived at your village, the one called Galeras saw me climb on the back of his horse...that big, gray one. He yelled at me with much anger! I jumped down and he hit me...my face! Blood came out of my nose and mouth, and I ran from him!" Blue Stone Shining stopped to sip water and then continued, "I ride all the other horses, though. It is faster when I am bringing them back from water or grass and the Spaniards want me to hurry." He grinned at Running Antelope. "Perhaps if you help me take care of the horses, the white-faces will let you ride!" Then with a chuckle he added, "Just remember to stay off the big gray one!"

И И И

As the sun approached the mountains to the west, Two Snakes stopped on a rocky ridge and waited for Galeras and the officers to join him. He pointed to the tops of cottonwood trees that peeped above the edge of a deep wash not far ahead. "We will find water there," he said to Gray Fox Comes Out, "and shelter from the wind."

"I see the trees," said Captain Cárdenas. "Find us a campsite, Galeras," he ordered. Galeras rode up to the wash, then to the right along its edge while gazing into it. He soon turned and waved, beckoning the others to follow, then disappeared into the deep watercourse.

И И И

Running Antelope helped Blue Stone Shining gather the horses and walk them downstream a short distance. The Spaniards had looped a short length of rope around each horse's neck after removing saddles, bridles, and the loads of food and personal items. The boys picked up the ends of these ropes and led the horses away, each taking two at a time. They allowed the animals to drink from the small stream, and then tied their individual ropes to either side of a much longer rope they had stretched between two cottonwood trees and tied securely to branches.

When all thirteen horses had been watered and tethered, the boys walked back to the encampment that now straddled the stream. "We get corn for the horses from the Spaniard called Gomez," said Blue Stone Shining, heading toward two cavalrymen who were sitting on bedrolls near the western edge of the wash. They had removed their helmets, steel vests, and heavy shirts, and were sipping water and talking. When they saw the boys, one of them pointed to a canvas bag next to a shallow fire pit they had dug. The bag looked to be full and was tied closed with a drawstring.

Blue Stone Shining nodded to the Spaniard and picked up the bag. Turning to Running Antelope he said, "We will give each horse some corn. Then we take them to where there is grass. Gomez will show us."

И И И

"The horse takes it from my hand!" Running Antelope cheered in surprise when he fed the captain's stallion its first small ear of corn. "It does not try to bite me!"

"That one will try to get more from you," Blue Stone Shining chuckled when the horse nuzzled against Running Antelope.

"Here is some more!" Running Antelope said, moving away from the animal's searching muzzle and holding out another yellow ear.

"It can have two more," advised Blue Stone Shining, reaching deep into the canvas bag, "and then it will have to fill its big stomach with grass."

Before returning the empty bag to Gomez and getting grazing instructions, the boys crossed the stream to the fire pit Gray Fox Comes Out had dug in the sandy soil near a cluster of cottonwoods. He had already started a small fire, and had gathered enough large sticks to keep it going for a while. "You have been with the horses," the old man said in greeting. "Two Snakes went off with his rabbit stick. He promises us a tasty stew for our meal."

"The horses have had water and corn, my uncle," Blue Stone Shining replied proudly. "It is done easily with Running Antelope helping me. Now we must take them to grass. When we return, we will help you eat that tasty stew!" Then, to Running Antelope he said, "If we take our rabbit sticks with us, we can practice throwing!"

Cavalrymen Gomez followed the boys back to the horses. He had put on his shirt and now carried a musket over one shoulder. "That big stick weapon he carries," Running Antelope whispered to Blue Stone Shining, a look of uneasiness on his face. "It makes thunder and sends out something that kills!"

Blue Stone Shining nodded, a concerned look on his face. "When grass is to be found away from the white-face camp, he comes with me carrying that big stick weapon. I heard its thunder many times when they fought with our warriors at Hawikú. I heard it on this journey, too, when a deer was killed."

Running Antelope shook his head, a sudden feeling of sadness causing his eyes to tear. "I heard the thunder, too," he said softly, "at Kawaioukuh."

When they reached the horses, each boy untied one end of the tether rope. Blue Stone Shining pulled the string of horses behind him as he followed Gomez to a well-worn path in the east side of the wash that took them back up to the desert floor. Running Antelope held on to his end of the rope and walked behind the big animals.

"There is plenty over there," said Gomez, pointing to a wide strip of knee-high desert grass growing along the edge of the wash a short distance to the north. Upon reaching the grass, the boys dropped the ends of the rope onto the ground allowing the horses to graze and wander within limits. Gomez sat down on a large rock, the butt of his musket on the ground and the long barrel pointing skyward. "You two can do what you want," he said to the boys, "but when I call you, get over here fast."

Blue Stone Shining nodded his understanding and relayed the message to Running Antelope. Then he asked, "Do you want to throw rabbit sticks?"

Running Antelope was gazing to the north at a broad mesa some distance away. "Do you see the smoke up there?"

"Yes, I see it."

"It comes from a village like mine. Its people are like my people." Running Antelope paused, remembering his father and journeys they had taken in this direction. "My father took me there." Then shifting his attention back to his friend, "Yes! We can find a thick bush to throw at." With a laugh he added, "One big enough that we cannot miss!"

И И И

It was almost dark when the boys returned to the campsite. Two Snakes and Gray Fox Comes Out were sitting by the fire pit talking with hand signs as well as words. Two Snakes greeted them first. "You have fed the giant dogs without them eating you!" he said with rare humor in his voice.

"Yes!" Running Antelope replied with enthusiasm. "They ate corn from our hands and followed us where we wanted them to go!"

"You both have done well today," said Gray Fox Comes Out. "Sit with us. We are about to eat." He nodded at a large bowl of stew sitting on a bed of coals to one side of the fire.

Running Antelope licked his lips in anticipation. "I am hungry for rabbit stew!" he said, leaning over to get a good look at the steaming mixture of cornmeal, water, crumbled piki, and chunks of fire-roasted rabbit meat.

"It is ready," said Two Snakes, reaching for the warm bowl with both hands and moving it to a flat rock he had placed between Gray Fox Comes

Out and himself. The boys sat down forming a circle around the meal. The two men each scooped out a mouthful of the thick stew with their fingers. The boys promptly did the same. The four continued to eat in silence until the bowl was empty.

"That was good!" said Blue Stone Shining while still chewing his last mouthful. "I tasted onions!"

Two Snakes smiled and nodded. "I put in onions that I found growing where the first rabbit was waiting for me."

"That was tasty stew!" agreed Running Antelope, licking his fingers. "Like you said it would be!"

Two Snakes nodded, a pleased look on his face, and reached for the empty bowl. Running Antelope's hand got to it first. "I will clean it!" He took the bowl to the stream where he allowed the current to wash away food remnants. When he returned to the fire pit, Blue Stone Shining was already stretched out beside it with his eyes closed. The two men were feeding sticks to the dwindling flames and talking quietly with each other. So, he set the bowl down on the flat rock and walked back to the stream.

Upon reaching its edge, he scooped up a drink of water with both hands and then stood up to gaze at the night sky. It was cloudless and sprinkled with countless stars. A bright half-moon provided light as he walked leisurely downstream. Ahead a short distance, he spotted a sandbar turned white in the moonlight. It was in the middle of the stream temporarily separating it into two smaller streams. He wandered over to it, splashing through cold water the last few steps. Before sitting down, he buried his bare feet in the sand, still warm from the heat of the day. Resting folded arms on raised knees, he listened to the silence of the night, and then closed his eyes and prayed silently before drifting into sleep.

"Running Antelope!" came the whispered sound of his name bringing him back into consciousness. "Are you awake?"

Running Antelope looked up to see Two Snakes standing on the far side of the stream. "You have come to pray?" he asked as a greeting.

"No, I have come to speak with you away from the others." He crossed the stream and sat down in front of Running Antelope. "I want to speak about the white-faces." His voice was quiet, but firm. He seemed older than his twenty summers. "I want you to know why we have come with them."

Bewildered by these words, Running Antelope searched the dark eyes fixed on his, but found no clue. "What...what is it you want me to know?"

Two Snakes did not answer right away. He continued to look deep into Running Antelope's eyes, and then spoke slowly, his words harsh with bitterness. "The white-face with the ugly scar— the one called Galeras." He paused, forcing the words out as if they were painful to say. "He killed my brother! He killed your father! We have come with the white-faces to kill him!"

15

Running Antelope could not sleep. He sat by the fire throughout the night staring into its glow, occasionally adding a stick or two to keep its flames alive. At the sandbar, Two Snakes had intensified the shock of his initial words by describing the horrifying scene he had witnessed at Kawaioukuh. Both shed tears, and they had walked back to their campsite in silence, completely drained of their normal vigor. But thoughts persisted, racing continuously in Running Antelope's mind, not allowing him to even doze.

He was up and walking before dawn, heading back to the place where the horses had grazed the evening before. There he would greet Sun Father, and perhaps start to clear away the confusion and fear that was disturbing him. He stopped near the rock where Gomez had stationed himself and stood silently facing east. At the earliest light, he began his prayer. "Oh, Sun Father," he said in a husky whisper, "I thank Great Power for making you. Without you there would be only darkness. Without you there would be no life for my people. You want us to have life, and Great Power wants us to have life, so you journey across the sky...and we live!"

Running Antelope paused to clear the hoarseness from his voice, and to carefully choose his next words. "My father taught me that all things living are good and have spirit that comes from Great Power. He would say that about the white-face Galeras...the man who killed him." He paused again, tears forming in his eyes and a growing lump burning in his throat. "I...I must think the same as my father! I must...want Galeras to live...not die!"

He sat down on the large rock unable to continue. Covering his face with both hands, he let the tears come. It was not until he heard Blue Stone Shining calling him that he got to his feet and headed back to the campsite.

И И И

Sun Father had cleared the horizon when Galeras signaled that the column of horses and men was ready to go. Two Snakes led the way out of the wash, taking a well-used path angling up its west side. Turning to the northwest, he proceeded at a moderate pace, occasionally stopping to allow the slow-moving column to keep up with him. All of the cavalrymen were walking except the officers and Galeras. Each carried his long, heavy lance balanced on one shoulder, while the horses carried sacks of corn, squash, and melons.

The rough terrain was spotted with sagebrush, yucca, and cacti. The faint trail meandered among them, avoiding the highest of ridges and mounds, and the lowest of gullies and ravines. Another large mesa came into view on their right, and more were visible beyond it.

𝒩 𝒩 𝒩

Their campsite late that afternoon was in a wash below a large mesa that had been clearly seen since early in the day. The wash was deeper and much wider than the one they had left that morning. Before going down into it, Two Snakes pointed to the top of the mesa near its southern tip where wisps of smoke could be seen rising into the air. "People like our people live there," he said to Running Antelope who was standing beside him. "That is Oldest Village...much older than ours. My brother and I stopped there when we walked this way." He fixed his eyes on Running Antelope's, nodded as if he was trying to make a point, then descended into the wash.

While the cavalrymen unloaded packs and saddles, Running Antelope and Blue Stone Shining tied the long tether line to a pair of cottonwoods further downstream. When that was done, they returned to the campsite and watched Gomez clean sweat and sand from his horse's coat with a thick-bristled brush about as long as his forearm.

"I like this horse," said Blue Stone Shining, reaching up to gently touch the big animal's cheek. It stood quietly next to them, its reddish-brown coat glowing more radiantly with each stroke of the brush. "I have ridden it more than any of the others."

Gomez stepped back to assess the results of his work, grunted his approval, and returned the brush to one of the saddlebags he had set on the ground. He rummaged around inside the bag with his hand and pulled out a smoothed cake of salt the size of a water gourd. "Give her a taste of this," he said to Blue Stone Shining, handing him the salt.

Blue Stone Shining received the salt with both hands and held it up to the mare's muzzle. The horse licked it eagerly. "It likes this better than the corn we fed it yesterday!" he laughed, his hands wet from the horse's tongue.

"Not too much," said Gomez. "Only a small amount each day. You can take her now." He handed Blue Stone Shining the end of the rope he had tied around the mare's neck and took back the cake of salt. "Let her drink some water."

Other horses were ready to be led to water, so the boys began the task of taking them downstream for a drink, then tying them to the tether. After the last horse had its drink and was secured, Blue Stone Shining walked over to Gomez's mare and untied it from the line. He led it over to the side of the wash where a grove of trees and a thicket of bushes blocked the view of the campsite. He stopped the horse beside a large, rounded rock and then looked back at Running Antelope with a wide grin on his face. "Do you want to get on its back?"

Without hesitation, Running Antelope hopped up onto the rock. His shoulders were now as high as the horse's back. He grabbed handfuls of hair from its mane, as he had seen Blue Stone Shining do, and swung his right leg up and over as he pulled himself on to its back. The big animal stood patiently, flicking its pale yellow tail to discourage buzzing flies from getting too close. "I like it up here! I am tall now!"

Blue Stone Shining handed him the end of the rope and stepped back. "Use your legs to tell it to go. Press them against its sides. Hold the rope behind its head, but do not pull on it."

Running Antelope followed his friend's instructions and the horse walked forward. "How do I tell it to stop?"

"Lean back a little, and pull gently on the rope."

"I like this horse, too!" Running Antelope cheered as the horse stopped.

"You can learn more on your next ride. We must go back now. There is no more corn for the horses, so we must take them to where there is much grass."

א א א

The evening light was dimming rapidly when the boys got to their own campsite. "I rode on the back of a horse!" Running Antelope announced to Two Snakes and Gray Fox Comes Out as he and Blue Stone Shining sat down with them next to the fire pit.

Two Snakes looked up in surprise, and then smiled and nodded his head approvingly. Gray Fox Comes Out chuckled. "You are like Blue Stone Shining with those horses!" He chuckled again. "He would eat and sleep on the back of a horse if he could!"

They all laughed, then turned their attention to the two bowls of food Two Snakes was placing before them. "We have *moho* with our stew," he said proudly, his fingers tapping the edge of the steaming bowl of reddish, banana-shaped yucca fruit. "I put these in the coals before Gray Fox Comes Out put his rabbits over the fire."

The four ate ravenously, nodding and grunting their approval of the meal as they chewed. Nothing was left behind in either bowl. Running Antelope sat back and sighed contentedly, patting his full stomach with both hands. "That was good!" He turned to Two Snakes. "Thank you." He had other thoughts he wanted to voice to Two Snakes...but not in front of his new friends...and not when he felt so drowsy.

"You look like you are almost asleep!" said Blue Stone Shining, nudging his friend with an elbow.

"I am...almost asleep," Running Antelope yawned. Without saying another word, he emptied his blanket-sack of belongings and put on the rabbitskin vest. Wrapping the blanket around him, he curled up beside the fire and closed his eyes.

И И И

By noon the next day, the high, rugged mesas and the vast shale and sandstone plateau that had sent them forth were behind the slow-moving column. Stretched before the travelers was the sun-drenched desert, its look of flatness as misleading as the shimmering blue illusion of water off in the distance.

"We are now following Sun Father's path!" Two Snakes called back to Running Antelope. "The Mountains of the Katsinam will now be our guides!"

"I see them!"

"We will keep them in front of us until we reach the Little River That Joins The Great Red River." Nodding to his left, Two Snakes added, "Blue Rock is a guide to the south!"

Running Antelope gazed at the distant tower of rock enveloped in blue haze. "I see it, too!"

"And to the north is Turtle Shell, the rounded hill you see over there!"

"I see it!" answered Running Antelope, reminded of his first journey this way...and his father's words about using such landmarks as guides.

It was late afternoon when Two Snakes unexpectedly signaled those behind him to stop, and abruptly dropped to one knee. He motioned for Running Antelope to join him, holding his gaze straight ahead. Running Antelope, bending low, quickly caught up with his friend and dropped to one knee beside him. "Antelope!" whispered Two Snakes. They were both looking ahead to a sandy plain dotted with clusters of sagebrush and sparse patches of ankle-high grass where a small herd of antelope was grazing. "I see one male and maybe ten females with their young," he continued. "I would like Gray Fox Comes Out to tell the white-faces. Perhaps we can all have the meat of our antelope friends for our next meal!"

Running Antelope hurried back to Gray Fox Comes Out, motioning to Blue Stone Shining to come with him. The three approached Galeras and the officers, who had stopped the rest of the column, and Gray Fox Comes Out spoke to them.

"Tell the three men with muskets to come up here," Captain Cárdenas said to Galeras as he dismounted. "They can go hunting with these natives."

The musketeers, led by Gomez, responded quickly and followed Gray Fox Comes Out and the boys back to Two Snakes. Bending low, they all followed Two Snakes as he moved off to the left a short distance, then stopped while he rechecked the direction of the afternoon breeze.

Running Antelope felt the wind on his face when he looked again at the grazing herd. Most were nibbling at sagebrush, even the fawns which were well along in growth. The single buck, its magnificent antlers reaching toward the turquoise sky, paused frequently to sniff the air and gaze about.

The hunters spread out facing the buck and its band. Running Antelope, with Two Snakes on his left and Blue Stone Shining and the others on his right, moved slowly forward, his bowstring fitted with an arrow. He fixed his eyes on the deer-like animals, watching for indications of their awareness of danger. *I am named after you, antelope friends,* he said in his thoughts. *I know you run faster than the fastest of men.* He did not notice the white hairs on the buck's rump raise. Two Snakes did. He stood up and let loose an arrow at the nearest doe just as the buck bolted. As the arrow struck, a volley of thunderous explosions came from the muskets and the bleating animals laid back their ears and took flight.

Running Antelope had let loose his arrow, but the deafening boom of the muskets had startled him so that it arced harmlessly over his fleeing target.

Blue Stone Shining had a similar experience. "My arrow hit a bush!" he said with a laugh. Gray Fox Comes Out simply shook his head and returned his arrow to its quiver. Two does lay dead where the antelope had been, one killed by an arrow, the other by a musket ball. The hunters walked over to examine them, each musketeer good-naturedly claiming credit for one kill. Two of them picked up their doe by its legs, and the three men continued to argue and laugh all the way back to the column.

Two Snakes bent down over the doe he had killed and adjusted its body so that the head faced east. Opening the pouch at his waist, he took from it a handful of sacred cornmeal and sprinkled it over the animal. He talked to it as he removed the arrow and allowed drops of its blood and bits of flesh to fall on the ground. "Thank you for giving me your life. I know that its value is the same as my life—that we are all one life under the sky. A life such as yours must sometimes be given up to another life such as mine. I hope that I have your permission for this killing."

ᴎ ᴎ ᴎ

That night was spent alongside a trickle of a stream just beyond the sandy plain, and all were up at dawn the following morning to prepare for the new day's trek. They traveled until the sun was just above the purple-black silhouette of mountains against the western horizon. Their camp that fourth night was next to a spring whose water gurgled out of the rocky ground beneath the branches of a solitary ironwood tree. The spring maintained a small pond while feeding an underground stream. Upon arriving there, Running Antelope had seen a flock of turkey vultures fly off, having had their use of the pond interrupted. Nearby, a pack of coyotes also had their watering plans changed and remained a respectful distance away, barking and yipping at the intruders.

"Tomorrow, no place to get water," Two Snakes informed his friends. "The white-faces should know that, too," he added, looking at Gray Fox Comes Out. "The day that follows will end with water again."

ᴎ ᴎ ᴎ

It was noon on the sixth day when the thirsty horses and men reached another wash. It was wide, but not deep. A man could stand in it and his head would be even with the desert floor. Its southbound stream was as wide as two horses standing one behind the other, and in some places almost as deep as a horse's knees. Captain Cárdenas gave the order to remain there overnight.

"The white-face chief wants to know how much farther to the Great

Red River," said Gray Fox Comes Out as the four of them rested in the shade of willow trees.

Two Snakes chuckled, shaking his head. "Six days to the Little River That Joins The Great Red River. Another four days to the Great Red River." He shook his head again. "If we did not have the white-faces slowing us down, we would see the Great Red River in three days!"

16

Running Antelope sat contentedly on the back of a horse and watched it lower its head to bite off more grass. It was an ivory-white mare with black markings over much of its body, and he held its rope loosely, giving it freedom to graze. Since leaving the wash encampment four days ago, he had ridden this horse each evening in search of adequate grasslands.

This evening, Gomez had spotted a grassy plain within view of the campsite. He rode his mare, and was armed with his sword and dagger, and a pistol borrowed from Captain Melgosa. Blue Stone Shining was on a lively, light-brown stallion, another one of his favorites. A tether line kept the other ten horses together.

"I have learned much from this horse!" Running Antelope declared when Blue Stone Shining rode up beside him after dropping the tether line.

"And we both have more to learn! I want to know how fast they can run!"

"Or if they can run at all!" Running Antelope chuckled, reaching over to pat his horse below its white mane. He glanced up when a shout rang out from the camp. He could see Galeras motioning to them and yelling to get their attention.

"Galeras wants us to go back!" called Gomez from the other side of the grazing horses. "They must have found water!" The boys slid off their horses, picked up their respective ends of the tether line, and easily swung themselves back on the big animals. Blue Stone Shining led the string of horses as he followed Gomez toward the campsite, and Running Antelope came along behind.

The shortage of water had become a serious problem, with a dry camp last night and again this evening. After the boys secured the horses between two tall cholla cacti and helped Gomez carry his saddlery into camp, they followed him to a dry streambed where Two Snakes, Gray Fox Comes Out, and several cavalrymen had been digging holes under the direction of Galeras. Four holes were now located along the dry bed five or six paces apart. They were large enough for a boy to stand in up to his waist, and at the bottom of each was a small pool of brownish water. "Gomez! Each horse gets one!" barked Galeras, pointing to the edge of the streambed where several large gourds had been placed. Running Antelope recognized them as containers the Spaniards used to carry water for their horses.

Gomez motioned for the boys to join him. "Each of you carry one—carefully—and come with me." Running Antelope used both hands to carry the heavy gourd he picked up. The boys followed Gomez to the campsite where he pulled two earthenware basins out of a canvas pack before moving on to the tether line. The cavalryman stopped in front of his horse and set one of the large bowls on the ground. "Pour the water into the bowl," he instructed, looking at Running Antelope and pointing first to the gourd and then to the pottery basin. The thirsty horse began to drink as soon as Running Antelope started to pour. Gomez set the second bowl in front of the next horse in line and motioned for Blue Stone Shining to pour from his gourd. As the horses drank, he pointed at the empty containers and said, "Now take these back and get two more."

The boys repeated the process, giving two horses water while cavalrymen refilled empty gourds. Running Antelope wanted to stop for a drink from one of his own water gourds, but he knew he would have to wait.

"Only one more horse!" Blue Stone Shining was finally able to cheer as the boys hurried back to the streambed with empty gourds. "Which one of us will carry its water?"

"I will!" Running Antelope called out, racing ahead.

"I can do it!" Blue Stone Shining yelled, chasing after his friend.

Running Antelope slid to a stop next to several full gourds. He grabbed one by its neck as Blue Stone Shining slid into him. The gourd flew out of his hands and tumbled onto the sand, its water gurgling out as both boys sprawled on the ground next to it.

Galeras strode over to them, a scowl on his scarred and bearded face. He grabbed each boy by an arm, yanked them to their feet, then smacked each one on the back of the head with an open hand. "Gomez!" he yelled as the two again sprawled on the ground. "Come get your *moqui* boys before I drown them in one of these water holes."

The cavalrymen laughed. Gray Fox Comes Out remained silent, a distressed expression on his face. Two Snakes glared at Galeras, his narrowed eyes glinting with hatred, and his fists clenching and unclenching.

⋈ ⋈ ⋈

Running Antelope had never experienced being hit by an adult. He felt bewildered by it, and angry, too. Also, his head ached the rest of the evening, and he had difficulty going to sleep. *Perhaps Two Snakes is right in what he wants to do,* he thought while lying awake under the stars. *No, he is not right,* he countered. *That is not the way of our people.* His thoughts continued to wrestle with each other until sleep finally came.

⋈ ⋈ ⋈

It was almost noon the next day when the gaits of the lead horses increased to a trot without direction from riders. "Maybe they smell water!" said Captain Melgosa as he and the others reined in their excited mounts.

"I hope you are correct," responded Captain Cárdenas, standing up in his stirrups to get a better view of the terrain.

"There is water ahead!" Two Snakes called to those behind him.

"I see a stream!" Running Antelope yelled, catching a glimpse of it between two grassy mounds. It was no wider than one long jump and was falling down stair steps of rocks toward the southwest. As the news spread throughout the column, shouts and cheers from the cavalrymen could be heard. "Since early this morning, I thought we were walking down a long slope," he called to Two Snakes. "Not a steep one, but one like on new corn—from the larger end to the smaller end."

"Your thinking was right," Two Snakes confirmed, pausing to let Running Antelope catch up with him. "We will follow this stream to lower lands where it meets the Little River That Joins The Great Red River. Tomorrow night, we will make our camp alongside those waters."

⋈ ⋈ ⋈

The Little River That Joins The Great Red River has its beginnings as cold, clear tricklets of water high up in forested mountains a two or three day climb south of Hawikú. Forming into a stream, it tumbles northward gathering other streams and small rivers as it rushes around rolling hills and across green meadows. Turning toward the northwest, it broadens when it reaches the colorful desert, and its color changes to the reddish-brown of the fine sand it begins to collect. It meanders most of its great length across the barren land, surging and foaming when fed by downpours of rain, and moving lower and slower in periods of dry weather. As it approaches its final destination—the Great Red River—it cuts an ever-deepening bed in the sedimentary rock beneath it, resulting in higher and steeper banks on both sides.

Running Antelope and Blue Stone Shining stood on the high northern bank of the river, enjoying the cool temperature of the morning and the view of the wide riverbed that was mostly sun-baked mud. The dry, cracked silt was colored the same reddish-brown as the waters that deposited it, which now snaked along as not much more than a wide stream. They had arrived there in mid-afternoon and camped overnight close to the high bank where the stream they had followed joined the river. Since Captain Cárdenas gave orders to remain there an extra day, and the horses were safely grazing next to the camp, the boys were now free to play and explore.

"My people have come to this river to find turtles," said Running Antelope. "The shells are used to make rattles. I have danced with one tied to my leg."

"We can see if there are any along here! I have found them in rivers near my village!"

The boys ran the short distance to the intersecting stream and then followed it upstream until they could easily climb down into its bed. They used the streambed as a natural path back down to the riverbed. There, they walked along a mud flat to a wide part of the riverbed's water flow—about 20 paces across—and waded in up to their knees.

"The mud goes between my toes!"

"Mine, too!" laughed Blue Stone Shining. "We want to go out to the middle. If we walk slowly, the turtles will not be afraid!"

"If there are any turtles!"

"Yes, if there are any—Ai! There is a step here!" Blue Stone Shining cried. "It is deep!" He was now up to his waist in the slow moving river. "Can you swim?"

"No! Can you?"

"No, but maybe I will soon learn!" They both laughed. "I can feel the water trying to push me! We should face into it so it does not push us far!"

Running Antelope walked cautiously until he was standing beside his friend. "Now what do we do?"

"Watch me! I will get on my knees and crawl along the bottom. If I see a turtle, I will grab it!"

"You will open your eyes down there?"

"Yes! Like turtles do! You can, too!"

"Try it! I will be watching!"

Blue Stone Shining faced upstream, held his breath, and submerged himself in the silty water. Running Antelope could see him crawling slowly forward, a dark shadow on the river bottom. When he pushed himself up to the surface, he stood gulping air and wiping his eyes. "I can see down there, but not very far!" he spluttered. "If I get close to a turtle, I can get it!"

"I will try!" Running Antelope declared before holding his breath and slipping beneath the surface. When he came back up he gasped, "I think I saw one! I saw something dark in front of me!"

"Did it move?"

"I ran out of breath before I could find out!"

"We can try it together! We can crawl beside each other and see more with four eyes!" Running Antelope nodded and moved alongside his friend. They took breaths and dropped to the bottom.

"I saw it!" shouted Blue Stone Shining when he raised his head out of the water.

"I did, too! It swam away fast!"

"They are fast! We have to be fast, too! Are you ready to try again?"

The boys spent the rest of the morning searching the river bottom for turtles and attempting to capture the few they saw. "I touched one!" bragged Running Antelope as he gave up and waded ashore.

"I had one in my hands, but it slipped away!" wailed Blue Stone Shining in disappointment.

"The Great Turtle Hunters will tell no one of their failure!" announced Running Antelope in a mocking tone.

"This will be a secret of the Great Turtle Hunters for the rest of their lives!" Blue Stone Shining thundered. Then, in a normal voice he asked, "Shall we go hunt something easier?"

Ⴡ Ⴡ Ⴡ

Running Antelope looked inside his blanket-sack and took two rolls of piki from the dwindling supply. He picked up his bow and quiver of arrows, and then joined Blue Stone Shining who was standing on top of a nearby mound gazing intently toward the northeast. "Have you seen anything yet?" he asked, tossing him a roll of piki.

"Not yet. We saw so many deer and antelope yesterday I could not count them. Now there are none to be seen."

"We saw some of the white-faces take their horses early this morning to go hunting. They may have caused the deer and antelope to run away." Running Antelope climbed to the top of the mound beside his friend and searched the rugged terrain with his own eyes. "We can follow the stream that led us here. It may now lead us to animals that drink its water."

Blue Stone Shining glanced at the sun that was midway on its course. "We must return to take the horses to water before the sun nears the mountains."

"We will," Running Antelope agreed before descending the mound in the direction of the stream. He led the way as the two began retracing their steps of yesterday, keeping the stream in view on their right.

"I see only lizards!" Running Antelope complained after they had walked a while.

"Lizards hunt and eat while other small animals stay in their holes, but large animals do not live in holes...and they will come for water!"

"If we see any, I do not want to kill," Running Antelope said solemnly, slowing to let his friend walk alongside him. "Two Snakes and Gray Fox Comes Out hunt to provide meat for our meals, so there is no reason for me to kill."

Blue Stone Shining nodded in agreement. "I will not kill either."

"But...we can see how close they will let us come to them!"

"And whoever gets the closest is the best Great Hunter!"

"Whoever gets the closest!" echoed Running Antelope. "That will be me!"

"No, that will be me!"

"We will see!"

"Yes, we will see!"

The two walked on in silence even more alert to their surroundings, including tracks and droppings left as evidence of animal journeys this way. After a while, Running Antelope raised his drinking gourd and pointed at the stream. Blue Stone Shining nodded, and they both turned toward the fresh water. The distant cry of an eagle caused Running Antelope to stop abruptly. "The eagle cries a warning!" he whispered to his friend. "It may be warning deer that we are here!"

The two moved slowly past clusters of sagebrush to within a few steps of the stream, then stopped again. On the far side and upstream a short distance were two deer, a small doe and her smaller fawn. They stood still, sniffing the breeze.

"The wind comes from behind them," whispered Blue Stone Shining.

"But they will see us if we move," cautioned Running Antelope. He took a small step forward and the deer glided noiselessly away, quickly hidden from view by tall shrubs. The boys crossed the stream and followed the imprints of the deer's split hoofs. Picking up speed, they were soon running through a maze of sagebrush, ironwood trees, and cacti.

"There!" Running Antelope called out, pointing at blurred movement to their right.

"There also!" shouted Blue Stone Shining, pointing to their left. "Oh-ee-e!" he cried out excitedly.

"Oh-ee-e!" Running Antelope screeched with glee. "Antelope! We found antelope! Run with them! We can run with them!" The two each chased after one darting, fleeing antelope after another. When one easily made its escape, another startled doe or fawn took its place.

"There are more over here!" shouted Blue Stone Shining, breathlessly, as he headed closer to the stream.

"Try to touch one!" Running Antelope cheered, turning in the same direction. "Oh-ee-e!"

The chase ended as unexpectedly as it had begun. The antelope were gone. The boys were breathless, as much from laughing and yelling as from running. "Did you touch one?" Blue Stone Shining asked, between gasps for air.

"No, but I came close one time!" Running Antelope boasted between breaths. "That was fun!"

"That was fun! I want some water, but I dropped my gourd when we started after the antelope. My arrows and bow, too."

"I did the same. Let us find them and go sit in the stream. We can drink and rest...and cool ourselves."

И И И

Sun Father was already approaching the mountains when the boys started back toward the Little River. "We have come far from the camp," observed Running Antelope. "Farther than I thought we would."

Blue Stone Shining glanced at the western sky with a concerned look on his face. "We must run again," he said, prompting both to quicken their pace to a jog. "We will need light to take the horses to water." They ran in silence, checking Sun Father's position every so often with increasingly concerned glances.

It was almost dark when they raced by the encampment and approached the line of tethered horses. Blue Stone Shining was about to untie one end of the tether line from a stout mesquite branch when the angry voice of Galeras rang out from the camp. "*Moqui*! The horses have had water! No thanks to you!" He was walking toward them, a scowl on his face and a wide leather belt hanging loosely from his right hand. Gomez was with him. "You failed in your duty today, *moqui* boy!" he growled, looking at Blue Stone Shining. "You will know better next time."

Running Antelope did not understand the words, but he recognized the contempt in the man's cold, gray eyes and scornful tone. He stepped back from the two white-faces, uneasy about their presence. He looked at Blue Stone Shining and saw fear in his friend's face.

"Hold him, Gomez!" Galeras barked. Gomez grabbed Blue Stone Shining by the wrists and turned him so that his bare back was in front of Galeras. Running Antelope cringed as the belt was swung. Blue Stone Shining gave a short cry as the heavy strip of leather raised an ugly welt across his back. He tightly sealed his lips to muffle his moans as the belt struck two more times.

"Now the other one!" Galeras snarled. It had not occurred to Running Antelope that he would be next until he was caught in Gomez's grip and pulled roughly over to Galeras. The belt stung him with pain beyond his experience. He tried to move out of the way of the second blow, but was held firm by Gomez's overwhelming strength. He cried out in anger, only to be silenced by the shock of the third lashing.

"Let him go!" Galeras ordered sternly. "Three is enough." His eyes squinted as he fixed his gaze on Running Antelope, and then Blue Stone Shining. "Three had better be enough, God help them!"

17

Sun Father had more then cleared the eastern horizon when Two Snakes led the column of Spaniards across the Little River That Joins The Great Red River. He had to take them upstream a short distance in order to climb out of the riverbed since its southern bank across from the encampment was almost vertical and as high as the head of a man on horseback. Once across, the column proceeded northwest alongside the river.

Running Antelope walked alone several paces behind Two Snakes, his mind filled with thoughts about the events of yesterday. *The plants-that-grow-on-rocks that Two Snakes put on my back have made much of the pain go away, but the skin of my back feels stiff like the hide of an animal hung up to dry.* He shrugged his shoulders slowly several times, wincing when the pain returned. *Stop thinking about your soreness! Think good thoughts instead...thoughts that will help the healing.* He switched his focus to the natural beauty of the morning all around him and put more energy into his stride. Turning his head, he glanced at Sun Father climbing higher in the sky. "Thank you for sending your warmth onto my back," he said aloud. "It feels good."

Off to his distant left, the deep purple Mountains of the Katsinam were silhouetted against a cloudy sky. He smiled, remembering the many times the Katsinam had visited his village during the past winter and spring—their last visit particularly—the day of the Going Home of the Katsinam. *There was much dancing and singing...and food and gifts,* he said in his mind, a*nd my father made a farewell speech inviting them to come back soon as rain.* His smile turned to a frown. *That was just a few days before we went to Kawaioukuh.*

Shortly before Sun Father would be midway in his travels, the column reached a deep wash, its rushing stream emptying into the Little River. Captain Cárdenas ordered a stop for resting and eating. Fresh food had run out several days ago, and every meal for the Spaniards was now roasted meat from whatever animals they killed, and cooked corn. Running Antelope and his companions fared better with wild rhubarb, yucca fruit, and fruit from the saguaro cactus, as well as their stews of cornmeal and roasted meat.

"Come with me," Two Snakes said to Running Antelope after they finished eating from a bowl of cornmeal mush. He nodded toward the wash, "We need to find a place where the horses can cross."

Running Antelope got to his feet and followed Two Snakes upstream along the edge of the wash. He saw that its bank would be easy for him to descend, but too high and steep for a horse. He also saw that the height of the bank gradually decreased the farther they walked, until it became no higher than a long step down to the sandy bottom. "We can cross anywhere along here and the horses can stop in the stream for a drink."

Two Snakes nodded in agreement. "Let us go across now." He stepped into the wash and headed toward the fast-moving water. "We can talk together on the other side without the ears of others hearing our words."

Running Antelope paused, wondering if the subject Two Snakes wanted to talk about was the one he had hoped had been forgotten days ago. With some reluctance, he followed his friend to the other side.

"How is your back?" Two Snakes asked when they reached high ground.

"It is much better," Running Antelope answered, trying not to show his discomfort about being there. "The plants-that-grow-on-rocks took away most of the pain during the night. I will heal quickly."

"The white-face Galeras showed you his evil ways again." Two Snakes paused, shifting his feet so he could look into Running Antelope's eyes. "We have waited many days to do what we came on this journey to do." His tone was harsh with deep-seated resentment. "We have waited so the white-faces will not likely go back to our village to seek revenge. They are tired and have little food, and I have made it known to them that following the Little River That Joins The Great Red River toward its source will easily take them back to Hawikú...with water to drink and animals to hunt all the way."

Running Antelope had to look away from the blazing intensity of his friend's angry eyes. When he looked back, Two Snakes continued in a more controlled manner. "We will soon reach the Great Red River. When the white-faces have seen enough, we will bring them back this way—and that is when Galeras will feel our arrows. You and I will then go back to the Great Red River and to the village of the Havasupai. I have friends there who will let us stay with them until we decide to return to our own village." He stopped talking, but continued to gaze into Running Antelope's eyes, as if expecting agreement.

Running Antelope returned the gaze, shaking his head slowly. "Revenge is not the way of our people," he said in a firm but quiet voice. "Our fathers and our grandfathers would tell us that we must not allow the evil ways of white-faces to cause us to be evil, too."

Two Snakes stepped back, his eyes narrowing as he stared unbelievingly at Running Antelope. "Galeras killed your father!" he snapped. "Does that not allow you to kill him?"

Running Antelope swallowed hard, and in a choked voice replied, "I cannot say that the ways of our people are right for everyone else but me. Our people are peaceful. We must be peaceful! If we were not, how could we offer our prayers with pure hearts? If our hearts are not pure, our prayers become weak. The Cloud People would forget us! There would be no rain! Our corn would die! Our people would starve!"

The two stood silently staring at each other until Two Snakes shook his head and stepped away. He walked back into the wash and crossed the stream without a return glance. Running Antelope, with tears forming in his eyes, watched his friend go. When Two Snakes was out of sight, he also crossed the wash and returned to where the Spaniards were preparing to move on.

И И И

The late-afternoon sun shone brightly on a grassy meadow bordered on two sides by outcrops of red sandstone from which water trickled. Captain Cárdenas selected a campsite there overlooking the wide, deepening riverbed. The afternoon trek had begun a gradual uphill climb that would soon steepen. "The men and horses will need their rest for the climb tomorrow," he said to Captain Melgosa. "You and I need our rest, too, for we will soon be walking instead of riding."

И И И

The next morning presented a cloudless blue sky and a chill breeze blowing down from the high country. The travelers got off to an early start, but at a noticeably slower pace. Some of the cavalrymen who had resumed riding their horses days ago as the packs of food became fewer, chose to walk their animals again as the ascent became steeper. Two Snakes showed increasing agitation with the slow progress, but said nothing to Running Antelope with whom he had not spoken since their emotional conversation back at the wash. He frequently stopped to let the Spaniards catch up with him, and would mutter to himself as he paced nervously back-and-forth waiting for them

By mid-afternoon, the Spaniards were ready to call an end to the day's climbing. Galeras found a campsite a short distance up another stream that flowed from the southwest into the Little River. Several low, twisted junipers offered shelter from sun and wind, and access to the stream was easy. Galeras, Gomez, and one of the other cavalrymen took the muskets farther upstream to hunt deer-like pronghorns that had been sighted earlier.

Ν Ν Ν

At noon the next day, Captain Cárdenas ordered a brief stop where he could view the Little River. When Running Antelope had the opportunity to join others at the overlook, he was surprised to see that the river was now far below them, with steep cliffs on both sides almost as high as the mesa where his village was located.

"Come see what has happened to the river!" he called to Blue Stone Shining as his friend approached him. "Tell me if you want to go hunt turtles today!"

"Hai!" cried Blue Stone Shining when he gazed down at the distant stream. "The turtles will have to find someone else to catch them. I have not yet grown wings to fly down there!"

Ν Ν Ν

The encampment that evening was some distance west of the deepening gorge. As Sun Father disappeared behind forested high country, the chill of the air forced Running Antelope to wear his rabbitskin vest as he ate a simple meal of cornmeal mush. He was tired from bringing water to the horses from a stream at the bottom of a deep ravine ahead of them. He had carried heavy water gourds up the steep trail more times than he could count.

"In the morning, we will have to continue west to find a place where the horses can cross to the other side," Two Snakes said to Gray Fox Comes Out as the two stood up to warm themselves by the campfire. "But before Sun Father draws near to his kiva tomorrow evening, we will see the Great Red River."

Ν Ν Ν

Late the next morning, the travelers arrived at a small pool of clear, cold water fed by an underground spring at the base of a light-gray limestone cliff. The rocky desert terrain was steep, and the view behind them verified the height they had climbed. "Look way out there and you can see the Little River

That Joins The Great Red River," Running Antelope said, pointing toward the southeast. "It is like a twisting snake coming after its next meal."

"I see it," Blue Stone Shining answered, shading his eyes with both hands. "We have come far since we played in its waters." Then, turning to nod at the pool, he added, "And this is the last water to be found as we continue to climb. I heard Two Snakes ask my uncle to inform the Spaniards. He said that we have to come back here each time we need more water."

"Does that mean that you and I will be carrying those heavy gourds again?"

"I do not know, but I feel tired just thinking about it."

With full water gourds packed carefully on each horse, the column moved forward and upward. The rough terrain was now sprinkled with low-growing juniper trees, their bent and twisted branches pointing in the same direction as the steady winds blowing down from the pine-covered plateau above. It was cold, and Running Antelope remembered his mother as he pulled his vest closer to him. "Thank you, my mother, for making this for me," he whispered. "Its rabbit fur keeps me warm."

The slow moving column reached the tree line as Sun Father descended behind tall piñon pines to their upper left. Soon, they were deep into thin forest on top of the plateau. "We have made it to the top!" Running Antelope declared. "But when will we see the Great Red River?"

Two Snakes glanced back at him, but said nothing. He motioned for him to pass and pointed in the direction they were heading. Running Antelope eagerly continued on, with Blue Stone Shining close behind. "If the Great Red River is so close to us, why will we have to return to the pond to get water?" Blue Stone Shining called out.

"I do not know..." Running Antelope started to answer as the forested tableland ended abruptly. There at his feet was the rim of the plateau—and beyond and below him a vast realm of flaming colors and deepening shadows beneath a darkening blue sky. Off to his left, Sun Father had arrived at the entrance to his western kiva, his rays of shifting light transforming the rich colors of land shapes while Running Antelope gazed in fascination. Yellows deepened to orange, pinks graduated to red, and pale, reddish purples darkened to royal purple. It was a sight well beyond his experience—beyond his imagination.

Blue Stone Shining broke the silence by whispering respectfully, "This must be the place of great spirits!"

"Look below us!" Running Antelope spoke louder, hardly able to contain his excitement. "Is that the Great Red River?" He was looking and pointing downward over the rocky edge of the plateau. "It looks so small!" Far below them—a distance he could not measure by comparison—was a narrow, reddish-brown ribbon of a river twisting and turning with seemingly easy flow at the bottom of a long, deep gash in the earth's surface. "That must be the river!" he affirmed, looking at Two Snakes for confirmation. Two Snakes nodded. Running Antelope returned his gaze to the bottom of the great canyon. "That is the Great Red River!"

18

The headwaters of the Great Red River are on the western slopes of a long chain of high, jagged mountains far to the northeast of the vast, colorful canyon that has captivated Running Antelope and Blue Stone Shining. They rise from countless clear springs whose streams naturally converge to define the river's southwesterly course across a vast plateau of broad uplands, wide valleys, and rugged canyons. Its many tributaries, including a major river from the north and another from the east, increase its size and volume to a powerful force as it approaches sedimentary layers of shale, limestone, and sandstone further to the southwest.

After turning west and merging with the Little River That Joins The Great Red River, the mighty flow cuts into the vulnerable sedimentary rock that awaits it. Over seasons too great in number for Running Antelope to comprehend, the persistent flood found its way into layer below layer of the compressed, hardened sediment, relentlessly wearing away particles and carrying them downriver to assist in further grinding and eroding.

In twists and turns, the Great Red River continues westward for a distance comparable to three journeys from Running Antelope's village to the south rim of its magnificent canyon. Its many rapids and waterfalls carry silt, sand, and gravel that have gradually deepened and broadened its channel while creating the spectacular canyon carvings that Blue Stone Shining sees as "a place of great spirits."

Not long after the Great Red River exits its creative masterpiece, it swings abruptly to the south and flows on for an even greater distance across desert lands and past ancient villages where extraordinarily tall men with long bodies are said to have lived. Finally, the river comes to an end where it empties into a saltwater sea.

Ν Ν Ν

Captain Cárdenas, a frown on his face matching the curve of his mustache that extended down both sides of his mouth to join the scraggly black hairs of his beard, had pulled his horse to a stop at the edge of the canyon rim and was looking down at the river far below. "There must be a way to get down there," he muttered loud enough for Captain Melgosa to hear.

The short, wiry Melgosa had swung down from his horse and now stood out on a shelf of rock that offered a better view of the challenge. "I see what might be an acceptable route if rope is used where it is otherwise impossibly steep." As an afterthought he added, "Climbing back up could be even more difficult."

"Have we seen any more likely place than this these past two days?" Captain Cárdenas asked in a tone of frustration.

"No, sir, we have not. This looks like our best chance right here." Melgosa gazed again at the river and swallowed hard. "From here, the river appears to be two or three paces across. From what our native guide is saying, it is really closer to a half a league wide." He paused and let out a long breath. "It could take more than a day just to get down there."

"Take what you need, then, and choose your companions. We will set up camp nearby and await your return. While you are gone, I will send Gomez and his *moqui* boys for a resupply of water...unless you want to take them with you!"

Captain Melgosa did not even smile at the words intended in jest. "I want Galeras to go with me...and Castillo," he said solemnly. "Both are strong men who are light on their feet."

"Very well. You have most of this day left, so get on with it."

И И И

Running Antelope had found much to like about the canyon side of this forest-covered plateau. He was awed each time he looked out at a colorful vista of stone sculptures rising from the canyon floor to practically touch the wispy clouds above. Each of the three mornings he had been here, he easily aroused himself before dawn and walked over to the plateau's edge to wait for Sun Father. Looking to his right, he would soon see a slight reddening of the eastern sky. The cold breezes from the north would noticeably die down, and Sun Father's first rays would stream silently across the great canyon. Dark shadows would give way to reddish purples, and then to reddish pinks. As Running Antelope prayed, the canyon brightened to a brilliant orange and Sun Father could be seen leaving his eastern kiva. *Thank you, Sun Father!* Running Antelope would conclude. *I am happy! I can greet you and my day begins!*

On this third morning, the dominant hues of the canyon's stone formations had again settled down to the familiar colors of ceremonial sashes frequently worn by the men of Running Antelope's village. There was the rich red of sandstone that stains the river, the flat sagebrush green of shale, and limestone's soft white, like the down feathers of an eagle.

Until now, the Spaniards had camped where they initially viewed the Great Red River. During the first day, they rode out from there toward the west along the canyon's south rim, searching the rugged, irregular cliffs for a way down to the river. On the second day, they extended their search further west with nothing to show for it but growing frustration. This morning, they were heading eastward from their campsite, frequently peering over the canyon's steep side for signs of a passage down. The words of Captain Cárdenas suggested that now they had found one. "Galeras!" he called out sharply. "Instruct Gomez to have the men prepare a campsite here, then you and Castillo report to Captain Melgosa. The two of you are going to accompany him down to the river!"

Galeras, who had dismounted and was gazing into the canyon, turned toward his captain with raised eyebrows, but said nothing. He shook his head imperceptibly and walked away to carry out his orders.

ᚠ ᚠ ᚠ

Running Antelope glanced curiously at Galeras and the two white-faces with him as he and Blue Stone Shining removed packs and saddlery from the horses. The three men had taken off their shiny vests and headpieces and tied water gourds and food bags to their wide leather belts. They were now standing near the plateau's edge connecting themselves with long stretches of rope secured around their upper bodies and under their arms. "What are they going to do?" he asked his friend.

"My uncle told me that they are going to climb down the long cliff to the Great Red River!"

"Can they do that?"

Blue Stone Shining shrugged his shoulders, an expression of uncertainty on his face. "I do not know. When we finish with the horses, we can go over there and watch."

"We should go now! All the white-faces are there, and so is your uncle and Two Snakes!" The two scampered over to where Gray Fox Comes Out and Two Snakes stood. Not far away, the group of Spaniards led by Captain Cárdenas had begun to call out words of encouragement as Melgosa, Galeras, and Castillo started their descent down a steep, narrow gully. The boys watched in fastenation as the three moved slowly and cautiously, grabbing for handfuls of brush for support whenever they slipped on loose rock.

"They found a path to walk on," Running Antelope quietly observed when the men reached a rocky ledge and filed along it toward another gully that would take them further down. The calls of encouragement continued, then stopped abruptly when Captain Melgosa dangled his body over a cliff and dropped out of sight. When he reappeared moving along another ledge, a loud cheer erupted from the men above, and then went silent again when Galeras dangled his body over the same cliff. Cheers greeted him when he could be seen again, then Castillo took his turn. Not long after that, the three could no longer be seen at all. Using the fingers of one hand, each Spaniard above silently outlined the figure of a cross near his heart, then turned away from the canyon and went back to routine tasks.

"The white-face Gomez is calling us," Blue Stone Shining said, interrupting Running Antelope's concentration as he continued to let his gaze search for the three climbers. "He wants us to go with him to the pond for more water."

И И И

Running Antelope was happy to be going to the small, spring-fed pool because he could ride one of the horses making the trip. Gomez allowed Blue Stone Shining and him to take the lead, each riding one horse and pulling two, as he kept watch from the rear. The boys let the horses set their own pace down the faint trail made by the feet of countless ancient people. They arrived at the pool when Sun Father was almost directly overhead.

When all of the water gourds had been filled and loaded on the four packhorses, the boys led the way back up the trail at a much slower rate. They reached the camp as Sun Father was nearing the western horizon, again turning the great canyon into a panorama of blazing colors. Shouts came from the Spaniards lounging around a large campfire kept burning during the day because of the cold. "Are they calling to us?" Running Antelope asked.

Blue Stone Shining hesitated, and then replied excitedly, "No! They are running toward the long cliff! The three white-faces have returned!"

Running Antelope could now see the three being greeted by the others and escorted into the campsite. "I would like to know if they reached the river," he said softly, more to himself than to his friend.

"It was difficult for us," Captain Melgosa said in a weak, raspy voice to those who gathered around him. He was sitting on the ground, his back against a piñon pine, sipping water from a gourd. "We must have gone down almost half way—at least a third. We stopped when we could go no farther. It was too steep! There was no way!" He paused to sip more water. "The river looks much bigger from where we were. The *moqui* who guided us here is correct about its size. It must be a half a league across, and the walls of rock on the other side are enormous! Bigger and taller than Seville's great tower!" He paused again and looked up at Captain Cárdenas who stood facing him. He sighed and bowed his head. "We went as far as we could."

Captain Cárdenas nodded, tiredness in his face. He was silent for a moment, and then shrugged his shoulders and let out a long sigh of his own. "We have all gone as far as we can," he said quietly. "We have found the river Coronado sent us to find. There are no cities, no villages—no people of any kind. This is a desolate, inhospitable land, cold enough to frost a man's bones!" His voice grew in volume and intensity. "We will leave this God-forsaken place tomorrow and return to Cibola!"

И И И

"I am happy we are going back to my village," Blue Stone Shining said as he walked briskly alongside Running Antelope. "It was too cold in the high land we left!" He shivered under his bisonskin vest. "I am still cold!"

"I am cold, too, but I am happy to have seen the Great Red River and the land of many colors that is its home." Running Antelope paused, thinking of his own home. "I would like to be going back to my village," he added wistfully.

Blue Stone Shining turned to glance at the line of Spaniards following closely behind his uncle. "The white-faces go much faster now that they all ride their horses. My uncle tells me that they want this journey to be over. Two Snakes could run if he wanted to and they would keep up with him."

Running Antelope pointed at the Little River That Joins The Great Red River off to his left. They were well beyond its deep gorge and it could be seen each time the trail took them up a sandy hill. "The Great Turtle Hunters will soon be able to hunt again," he did his best to say in a serious tone.

Blue Stone Shining wrinkled his nose in opposition to the idea. "The Great Hunters should hunt with bow and arrows, or throwing sticks," he responded firmly. "We are land hunters, not water hunters."

"Then let us do that before this day ends! We have yet to bring in meat for a meal."

И И И

It had taken less than two days to return to their first campsite on the Little River, but instead of stopping there, Captain Cárdenas chose to remain on the river's southern side and continue on some distance to where its bank was only a short step down to the riverbed. A campsite was established on a stretch of sparse desert grass along the bank's edge. After the boys led the horses to the river for water, they tethered them on grass downriver from the campsite. They then joined Grey Fox Comes Out, who was preparing a small fire pit just south of the horses.

"We will hunt rabbits for our meal, my uncle," Blue Stone Shining announced when the old man looked up and nodded his greeting.

"Darkness arrives quickly," he responded with a gesture for them to hurry, "and I am hungry!" he called after them as they darted off toward the southwest.

И И И

Running Antelope's bow was in his left hand, its quiver of arrows strapped firmly behind his right shoulder. Blue Stone Shining's right hand gripped one end of his throwing stick, leaving his left hand and arm free and loose to balance his body when it came time to throw. They slowed to a walk and advanced farther into the barren, rolling landscape of rock outcroppings, sandy soil, and scattered desert plants. "Over there," Running Antelope said quietly, nodding directly ahead at a cluster of low shrubs huddled around a lone saquaro cactus. "That is where I would be if I was a rabbit." He reached for an arrow and placed its notched end in the center of the bowstring, letting its shaft rest on the bow just above his left hand's grip.

"We will see if anyone is at home." Blue Stone Shining picked up a large stone and lobbed it into the plants. When it crashed, two startled rabbits scampered out into the open, and then stopped wide-eyed and motionless. Running Antelope squared his feet and brought his bow and arrow up. Pulling back the bowstring with fingers of his right hand, he aimed at the rabbit closest to him and let the arrow fly. At the same instant, Blue Stone Shining threw his heavy, curved stick at the other rabbit. Both boys held their breaths as one of the rabbits went down.

"I missed!" cried Blue Stone Shining. "The rabbit was just waiting there for my stick to hit it!"

122

"You can try again," Running Antelope said while sprinkling a pinch of sacred cornmeal over the dead rabbit's body. "It is waiting for you over there." He pointed at the rabbit, now crouched motionless next to a large patch of prickly pear cacti.

"I will get it this time!" Blue Stone Shining affirmed as he headed in the rabbit's direction.

Running Antelope caught a glimpse of another rabbit off to his far right. "I am going over this way!" he called to his friend while reaching for another arrow.

И И И

"Two rabbits for you and none for me!" Blue Stone Shining wailed when the boys met up again. "I should have brought my bow instead of this stick! I could not hit a rock today, even if I was sitting on it!"

"You can go back for your bow if you want to. If you take these with you, your uncle will have them over the fire when we return."

Blue Stone Shining thought for a moment before taking the rabbits and turning to leave. "If I run, my arrows might kill one or two before darkness comes!"

Running Antelope watched his friend dash off toward the river, then continued his hunt in the same direction. He walked slowly, pausing occasionally to toss a rock into a concentration of shrubs or cacti. An arrow was in place on his bow, ready to be released in the blink of an eye. So far, no rabbit had been close enough to warrant a shot.

Sun Father had begun to sink behind the Mountains of the Katsinam when Running Antelope heard men yelling from the direction of the campsite. Their tones sounded like calls of alarm. He stopped to listen just as the shouting became more intense and was punctuated by the unmistakable roar of a musket. The sharp crack of a pistol followed, then another thunderous musket blast. "Two Snakes!" he muttered under his breath before springing into a run toward the sounds.

The rough terrain prevented him from seeing the camp, but he knew it was not far away. He sprinted across an open stretch dotted with spiny ocotillo shrubs, then around a rock-strewn hill to a shallow, sandy wash. He ran along its dry streambed until he neared the camp's edge. Bounding out of the wash, he could clearly see Spaniards coming from the riverbed and gathering beside their campfire. *They speak with angry voices,* he said in his thoughts, noting their tones and gestures. Off to his left, he saw Blue Stone Shining and Gray

Fox Comes Out standing near their campfire. They were waving and calling to him with looks of concern on their faces. *Why do they want me to put my bow down?* he asked himself. He started to head their way when he heard more shouting from the Spaniards. *The white-faces are yelling at me!* he told himself when he looked in their direction and saw several pointing at him. He stared in disbelief when Galeras stepped away from the others, raised a musket to firing position, and aimed its long barrel at him. *He wants to kill me with the stick weapon!*

The musket thundered in a cloud of smoke as Running Antelope turned and ducked low to the ground. He heard the whine of the musket ball passing close over his head before he plunged back into the wash. His legs could not carry him fast enough as he raced back up the streambed and then darted out of it to put the rocky hill between him and the Spaniards. He did not stop. Back into the rough, desert terrain he raced until it was almost too dark to see where he was going. Coming upon a shallow arroyo choked with mesquite, he jumped into it and crawled under the spiny shrubs until he could crawl no farther. He lay there, breathless and shaking, his heart throbbing in his heaving chest. "He wants to kill me!" he gasped. "The white-face Galeras wants to kill me!"

19

A crescent moon was slowly rising from the southwest to offer its small amount of light as Running Antelope lay motionless in his crawlspace among the mesquite. He had been listening intently for sounds of pursuers, but so far had heard nothing. Satisfied that no one was chasing him, he backed out of the thicket and stood up, his eyes and ears fully alert. *I must go back to my village! I want to be with my family and my friends!* He took a few cautious steps as the reality of his situation became clearer to him. *I need to get my blanket! It has my warm vest in it, and my gourds and fire rocks! Without them, I will not live to see my village!* He walked on in the direction he knew would take him again into danger.

Stopping frequently, he looked for signs of movement around him, and listened for sounds that could signify a threat. *The wind blows now*, he told himself. *It hides the sounds that others make. I must be careful!* Recognizing the dark outline of a rocky hill to his right, he said in his mind's voice, *The river is not far. I will...*He stopped and dropped to one knee. Reaching behind him, he pulled an arrow from its quiver and armed his bow. *Something is moving near the hill!* He stared into the darkness trying to determine what he was seeing. Pulling back the string of his bow, he was about to take aim when he heard his name called out in a voice not much louder than a whisper. "I am here!" he called back, relieved to see Blue Stone Shining approaching him from the darkness.

"I have been looking for you since the moon showed part of its face!" Blue Stone Shining exclaimed in an excited whisper as the two gripped each other's arms. "Have you been hiding with the rabbits in their burrow?" he added in a feeble attempt at humor.

"I have been hiding to save my life!" stormed Running Antelope. "Why do the white-faces want to kill me?"

"Let us move out of the moonlight and I will tell you. The white-faces are not searching for you, but if one should have to take a walk in the dark, we do not want him to see us."

The boys found a small boulder near the base of the rocky hill and sat down with their backs against it. "Why do they want to kill me?" Running Antelope asked again, his voice choked with emotion. "I have done nothing!"

"It is because of Two Snakes! He tried to kill the white-face Galeras! My uncle and I saw him! He came out from behind the horses and stood close to the white-face camp, his bow and arrow ready. Some of the white-faces saw him and called out to the others as he pulled back his arrow. Some threw themselves to the ground! Galeras was one, and the arrow passed so close to him he must have heard it whisper his name!"

Running Antelope let out a long sigh and shook his head slowly. There was a catch in his voice when he asked, "Did...the white-faces kill Two Snakes with their stick weapons?"

"They tried to," Blue Stone Shining said with a chuckle, "but Two Snakes runs like a deer. When his arrow missed Galeras, he turned and ran along the river toward the last light. It was soon too dark for him to be seen."

"So the white-faces decided to kill me instead!" Running Antelope snapped.

"They saw you with your bow—and an arrow ready to draw back! They thought you were going to kill one of them! My uncle and I called to you to put down your bow, but you did not hear us!"

"I heard you, but it was too late!" Running Antelope moaned. "Now I must leave here or be killed!" He paused, shaking his head, and then added, "My blanket is near your uncle's fire! I must have it for the journey to my village!"

"I will get it for you," Blue Stone Shining assured him, rising to his feet. "The white-faces will not see what I do. They will stay close to their fire to keep warm and will soon sleep. You can stay here. I will come back with your blanket."

Running Antelope nodded and smiled gratefully as he watched his friend disappear into the darkness. His thoughts now turned to the journey ahead of him. *I will go back down the river to the stream that enters where we hunted turtles. I will go up the stream and follow it as far as I can, then go on toward Sun Father's kiva to the east. His path will guide me to my village.*

ᴎ ᴎ ᴎ

It was not long before Running Antelope's planning was interrupted by the return of Blue Stone Shining. "Here is your blanket!" he said proudly. "I put your throwing stick and gourds inside it. The white-faces did not even look at me!"

"Thank you for doing that," Running Antelope said, relief evident in his voice, "but why did you bring your own blanket, too?"

Blue Stone Shining grinned and sat down beside Running Antelope using the blanket-sack slung over his shoulder as a pillow against the boulder. "I would like to go with you," he announced still grinning, "if that is all right with you!"

"Yes! I want you to! But...what about your uncle?"

"My uncle agrees that I should go with you. He says the white-faces cannot be trusted. They could turn against any of us just as the wind changes. He will go back to Hawikú and then leave them."

"I want him to be safe!"

"It is his choice. I said to him that he could go with us, but he does not want to ride a horse."

"Ride a horse?" Running Antelope questioned, sitting up straight and staring at his friend.

"Yes! My uncle said we should take horses!"

"Why?" was all Running Antelope could say, a puzzled look on his face.

"We can go much faster!" Blue Stone Shining laughed. He then continued in a serious manner, "My uncle said that if we walk and one of us injures a foot or leg, we could not go on and would probably die. That would not be so with horses."

Running Antelope thought about his friend's words. "Your uncle is wise, like my father. If one of us got hurt and could not walk, it would mean death. But with horses to ride..."

"Then we will do it! When the white-faces are asleep, we will take two of the horses and ride like the wind to your village!"

И И И

The boys waited until the moon was hidden behind passing clouds before heading toward the horses. They crept silently past the glowing embers of the campfire near which Gray Fox Comes Out was sleeping. Off to their right, the fire in the white-face camp was kept blazing by the lone cavalryman on sentry duty. Pointing to him, Blue Stone Shining whispered, "He is blinded by the light of his own fire. He cannot see into the darkness."

The horses were tied to a long tether stretched between two iron stakes that Gomez had driven into the ground with a heavy rock. The tether was perpendicular to the nearby riverbed, with seven horses on one side of the line and six on the other. The boys quietly approached the animals on the downriver side.

"Here is the one you like," Blue Stone Shining whispered, pointing to the ivory-white mare with black markings that Running Antelope had frequently ridden. "I will ride this one," he added, stepping between horses to untie a light-brown stallion from the tether.

Running Antelope greeted his horse by stroking its flank and back, and then its neck. The mare nuzzled him as he reached down to untie its rope from the tether. He stroked the mare again and then led it away keeping the tethered horses between himself and the white-face camp. Blue Stone Shining was right behind him, leading the stallion. Because of the sandy terrain, it took only a short time for the horses' tracks to be erased by strong gusts of wind.

Running Antelope kept the lead, staying near the riverbank for a while before moving down into the channel and walking his horse on the dried mud. When a bend in the river blocked the view of the sentry's fire, he turned to look at his friend and gestured toward the mare with a movement of his head. He tossed his blanket-sack over the mare's back to hang on the far side. Still holding on to it with his right hand, and the mare's rope wound around his left wrist, he used fingers of both hands to grab hold of the horse's mane and swing himself onto its back. He set the blanket-sack in front of him and adjusted the position of his bow, which was fitted over his head and one shoulder. Glancing behind him to confirm that Blue Stone Shining was mounted on his horse, he pressed his legs lightly against the mare's sides. The animal responded instantly by moving forward at an energetic pace.

Running Antelope let the mare set its own gait and smiled broadly. He wanted to let out a loud yell, but instead simply shook his fist in the air. Blue Stone Shining rode up alongside him laughing, and they both shook their fists in the air.

"We can cross here," Running Antelope said before gently pulling the mare's rope against the left side of its neck. It responded by turning to the right and stepping into the river's moderate flow. After crossing, it needed little direction to turn left and continue downriver along the dried mud border. "Just ahead is where we caught all of those turtles!"

"I remember! We had to throw most of them back into the water because we could not carry them all!"

"You remember well," laughed Running Antelope, pointing off to his right, "and the little stream we followed to get to this place enters the river there!" He soon turned his horse to the right and let it slosh its way up the streambed. After a short distance, he reached over as far as he could and pressed his hand against the right side of its neck. The mare turned to the left, walked out of the stream, and bounded up a sandy slope to the desert floor.

א א א

The moon had climbed higher in the star-filled sky providing light for the travelers to find their way. The horses settled into a steady pace near the left side of the stream, the rhythmic sound of their hoofbeats muffled by the sandy soil. When their course around rocky outcroppings or patches of cacti or shrubs caused the boys to lose sight of the stream, the continuous murmuring of its flowing waters could still be heard. They continued on up the long, gradual slope of the broad plateau that awaited them, the silence of the night broken only by the yipping of coyotes and the stirring of the wind.

א א א

As dawn approached, Running Antelope once more rubbed his eyes and shook his head vigorously. The rocking motion of his horse had been coaxing him to doze throughout much of the night, and this is how he had been dealing with the challenge to stay awake. Now, as the first signs of earliest light appeared in the east, he turned and called to Blue Stone Shining a horse-length behind him. "We can stop for a while and greet Sun Father...and wake ourselves up!"

His friend replied between yawns, "We can make...a small fire, too...and eat some warm stew."

"Stew? We have stew?"

"We have ground corn—and water to make warm over a fire—and a bowl to put it in!"

"What else do we have to put in it to make a real stew?"

"Nothing else. Only the ground corn."

"Then let us have stew for our meal," laughed Running Antelope. "We can call it *ground corn stew*!"

א א א

By the middle of the afternoon, hunger and sleepiness caused the boys to stop and prepare for the night. "I see large rocks ahead of us!" Running

Antelope called out. "They will shelter a fire from the night winds!"

"I see rabbits! They can help us make a real stew!"

"We need their help for that! My stomach is calling out to them!"

They soon reached the cluster of boulders and slid off the horses to look for a campsite. "It feels good to stand and to walk!" Blue Stone Shining said, following Running Antelope around the nearest boulder. "We might have to learn to walk again when this journey is over!" He laughed at the thought.

"There is room for the horses in here!" Running Antelope observed as he viewed the sandy floor of the enclosed area. "Our fire can be here!" He marked a place in the sand with the heel of his foot. "We need to find grass for the horses, and let them drink from the stream," he continued as if talking to himself. "And gather many sticks for a fire...and some dry grass to give it life from our fire rocks."

"And we must be great hunters and provide rabbit meat for our real stew!" chimed in Blue Stone Shining.

"We have much to do!"

И И И

Sun Father had reached the western horizon when the boys finished skinning the two rabbits their arrows had killed. They cut up the meat with obsidian knives and skewered the chunks on sharpened ironwood sticks. They then stuck the ends of the sticks in the sand close to burning coals. When the pieces of meat were well roasted, Running Antelope pulled some of them off the skewers and into the steaming bowl of cornmeal and water that Blue Stone Shining had set on hot coals. The boys remained squatted next to the shallow fire pit, licking their lips hungrily as they watched the steam rise from the simmering mix.

They shared the bowl of stew when it was ready, then prepared a second bowl just like the first and shared that. It was dark when they were chewing on the last few mouthfuls. "That was the best stew I have ever eaten!" Running Antelope declared with a sigh of contentment.

"Even better than your mother's?" Blue Stone Shining asked before he sat back, patting the bulge of his full stomach.

Running Antelope thought briefly before answering, "Just as good!" He smiled and nodded. "Just as good!"

20

"The stream we have followed begins over there!" Running Antelope called out. He pointed to a low ridge of exposed sandstone off to his right as Blue Stone Shining rode up alongside. "Water is coming out of the ground in many places." Along the base of the ridge, a steady flow seeped from several locations to feed streamlets that converged to form the stream. "I have one prayer stick left in my blanket. I will place it in wet sand when we fill our gourds."

"The next stream we see may be far away! When Two Snakes led us to this one, we had not found water for three days, except in the holes the white-faces dug."

"I have not forgotten. We may also have to dig for water, but we can go farther in a day than the white-faces did. We can start earlier, ride faster, and not stop until Sun Father is close to his kiva."

Blue Stone Shining smiled. "I like what you say!" He slid off his horse, reached into his blanket-sack, and pulled out three empty gourds. Looking over at Running Antelope who had also dismounted, he affirmed with a grin, "We will cross the dry lands before our gourds are empty!"

И И И

At midday, the boys stopped to allow the horses to graze in sparse grass, and to drink from the limited supply of water. There were eight gourds altogether, each as long as a boy's forearm, with a rounded bulge at the bottom and a corncob stopper.

"We can each keep a gourd for our own use," suggested Running Antelope, "and use the others for the horses. They have a greater thirst."

Blue Stone Shining nodded, and then pulled out the stew bowl and a full gourd from his blanket-sack. "I will empty this into the bowl for my horse, then you can use the bowl and one of your gourds for your horse."

И И И

They stopped again in mid-afternoon to give water to the horses, but with growing concern over the possibility of a dry camp that night. "We now have only one gourd left for each horse," said Blue Stone Shining as he poured water into the bowl. "We should stop soon to dig!"

Running Antelope sighed as a worried look came over his face. "You are right! We must stop soon, or there will be no water for our horses in the morning—or for us!"

и и и

Sun Father was low in the western sky when Blue Stone Shining called out, "If we do not find a digging place now, we will be digging in the dark!"

Before Running Antelope could reply, he was caused to hold the mare in check by firmly pressing its rope against the left side of its neck. "My horse wants to go to the left!" he laughed. "It must have forgotten that I want it to go straight."

"My horse wants to do the same! Their noses may be telling them where there is water!"

"Let us see where they take us!" Running Antelope held the rope loosely and the mare veered to the left at a faster gait toward the slope of a moderate rise. They were soon looking down from its crest at a hollow where a single yellow-leafed cottonwood grew among desert shrubs and rocks. "I see water down there!"

"It looks like a small pond!" Blue Stone Shining cheered as his horse caught up with the mare. "No digging for water today!" he laughed. "We can cross the dry lands with water left in our gourds!" The boys rode right up to the edge of the shallow spring-fed pool and remained mounted as the horses drank. They gazed upon the perfect desert campsite their animals had brought them to—plenty of water, a tree for shade, and protection from wind.

"Is that a fire pit over there?" Running Antelope asked, pointing at a ring of rocks on the other side of the pond. The boys slid off their horses and walked around the pond to see. "There are many footprints here! The winds have not yet covered them with sand!"

"This is a fire pit!" Blue Stone Shining called out as he stepped into the circle of stones. Dropping to his knees, he dug into the ashes with both hands. "Deep in the ashes it is still warm! People must have been here last night!"

"Some of the footprints are small, like those of women, or even children," Running Antelope said when he joined Blue Stone Shining. "There was another fire over there!" he added, pointing to a circle of rocks between two large boulders farther out from the pond. "Many people were here last night!"

"Who do you think they are? Could they be your people?"

"Not from my village—but perhaps from Oldest Village—or from a village near it where other clans of my people live. But I do not know why they would bring children with them this far away."

"If they are not your people, who could they be?"

Running Antelope took on a solemn expression as he gave thought to the question. "Old Enemies," he answered softly. "They could be Old Enemies."

"Who are they? And why would they be here?"

"Old Enemies do not live in a village. Their men do not plant corn or cotton. Their women do not make bowls or blankets. They do not live in one place. That is what my father told me."

Blue Stone Shining started to speak again, but instead paused as if to think some more. Then he asked, "Why do you call them *Old Enemies*?"

"Because they come to the villages of my people to steal corn and melons from the fields. My father said they sometimes attack a village and take what they want from the houses and kivas. They will take women and children, too, and kill anyone who tries to stop them."

Blue Stone Shining nodded his head slowly. "I understand," he said softly. "I have seen such people come to Hawakú to trade. My people call them *Strange Ones*. Some think of them as enemies, too. When they come to my father's trading house, he sends me away and speaks to them himself. At times, they have with them a woman or a child who they want to trade. Most traders in Hawikú are like my father and will not trade people, but there are some who will."

"I hope we never see the people who were here last night. I will be happy to leave this place and ride on to my village."

И И И

The boys left the pond early and were well on their way when Sun Father cleared the eastern horizon. The horses had eaten enough grass and consumed enough water to satisfy them for a while. Gourds were full, the sky was clear, and the chill of early morning was beginning to give way to the sun's warmth, but Running Antelope felt uneasy. He had not slept well, and was disturbed by his thoughts. "I keep thinking about Old Enemies!" he called out. "My father told me that the only way to treat them is to fight them. He never said that about anyone else."

"I think your father is right! They are cruel people who are never to be trusted. My father caught some of them stealing from his trading house, and when he told them to leave, they threatened to kill him!"

"I am not going to think about them anymore! I will keep my thoughts on good things instead—like getting back to my family!"

И И И

The two riders continued on across the broad, high ground of the plateau. They crossed long stretches of stony ground where few plants grew, as well as extended areas of sand where they had to pass over ridges and go around high mounds. In some places, grass grew in sparse patches, as did cacti and small bushes. The dry air became warmer as Sun Father climbed higher in the sky, and swirls of sand caught up in the wind rose from the dry land around them.

They stopped at midday to give each horse a gourd of water. While the animals nibbled at grass, Blue Stone Shining roasted pieces of a freshly killed rabbit over a small fire while Running Antelope searched for edible plants to put in their stew.

"I am hungry!" declared Running Antelope upon his return.

"It is because we did not eat this morning. I am hungry, too." Blue Stone Shining emptied his sack of cornmeal into the bowl still wet from the horses use. "This is all the corn we have left," he said with a frown. He added water from his gourd and stirred the gravy-like mixture with his finger before placing the bowl on hot coals. "The next meal we have with corn will be in your village!" He laughed before adding, "I will taste your mother's stew and decide for myself if the stew you make is as good!" As the mixture began to bubble, he forced the pieces of rabbit off their skewer and into the steaming bowl. Running Antelope dropped in the white, inner layers of wild carrots he had peeled, and then they waited in anticipation as the stew continued to bubble and steam.

И И И

"We have left the high ground behind us!" Blue Stone Shining called out as the beginning of a long descent from the plateau became noticeable.

Running Antelope twisted around to nod his agreement, then returned his attention to the view ahead. With his free hand, he shielded his eyes from the bright light of the afternoon and squinted as if to see in the distance more clearly. *Are those the tops of trees?* Twisting around again, he called to his friend, "Look far ahead of us! Do you see a long row of yellow that could be the tops of trees?"

Blue Stone Shining rode up alongside and bent forward as he peered into the distance. He raised a hand to shelter his eyes and peered again. "Yes!" he finally said. "Yes, it is a row of treetops! Yellow! There will be water for us there!"

"That is what I am thinking!"

"Will we be there before it is dark?"

Running Antelope turned his head to look at Sun Father over his right shoulder. "We will do our best! If the stream there is the one I am remembering, it is only two or three days beyond to my village!"

И И И

Sun Father was almost touching the Mountains of the Katsinam when Running Antelope leaned back a little and pulled gently on the rope. When his horse stopped, he relaxed the pressure on the rope and waited for Blue Stone Shining to move his horse up beside him.

"Are you stopping to give the horses their gourds of water?"

Running Antelope was staring ahead at the line of yellow treetops that had been clearly visible for quite a while. "I see smoke," he said, almost in a whisper. "We may have found Old Enemies."

Blue Stone Shining stared along the tops of the fall-colored cottonwoods. "I see the smoke, but it could be someone else," he said in a hopeful tone.

"How will we find out? If we get close enough to see them, they will see us!" The boys remained on their horses, deep in thought as they stared at the distant wisps of smoke. Running Antelope finally spoke again, "Whoever is there is camped inside the cut in the ground that the stream made. We could ride up to the edge of the cut and look down at them. If they are Old Enemies, we ride away quickly to the north. Later, we rest by the stream, then leave it behind us when morning comes."

Blue Stone Shining considered the idea, and then warned, "Their arrows could catch us when we are looking down at them."

"If they have never seen horses before, they will be afraid like my people were when the white-faces came to our village. They might even run away!"

"Will they be afraid if they see two boys on their backs?"

Running Antelope paused to think further. "Our blankets! We can cover ourselves with our blankets! It will be almost dark. They will think we are part of the giant dogs!"

Blue Stone Shining grinned at him. "We can cut holes in the blankets for our eyes to see! They will be too frightened to hold their bows steady!"

Sun Father had disappeared behind the mountains leaving only a small amount of his light in the sky when two shrouded figures on the backs of giant dogs rode up to the western edge of the deep, wide wash. Their presence was announced first by a chorus of anxious barks and howls from a dozen or so real dogs who dashed out from the shadows surrounding two campfires that burned brightly on the far side of the stream. The shouting of men and the screaming and crying of women and children quickly joined the yelps. As the fearsome creatures looked down upon them, the people ran in panic toward the eastern side of the wash. Some huddled there behind bushes and the trunks of trees, while others scrambled up the side of the wash and fled into the desert.

The boys gazed in awe at the scene of confusion unfolding below them. Soon, most of the people were out of sight. The few dogs that remained whined nervously as they paced up and down along the far side of the stream. The sounds of frightened people gradually died out. "We should leave now," Blue Stone Shining said in a hoarse whisper. "These people are enemies!"

Running Antelope was about to agree when he spotted a man standing alone near the pacing dogs. His arms were folded across his chest, and he stared up at the intruders with an unwavering gaze. He showed no fear. "Let us leave slowly," he whispered back. "Their chief is looking at us. He must not see fear in us."

The twilight rapidly turned to darkness as the boys rode north keeping the tree-filled wash on their right. An early moon provided enough light for them to direct their horses, but the pace was slow. It was well into the night when they considered themselves to be far enough away from the Old Enemies to stop. "Let us find a way down to the stream," Running Antelope suggested between yawns. "The horses need water and we need sleep!"

"I am ready! We can find grass for the horses when daylight comes, and perhaps a rabbit or two for our meal. Right now, I just want to sleep."

Moonlight glistened off the strip of fine, almost-white sand the boys had chosen for their sleeping places. The horses were watered and had been able to nibble at grass growing next to the stream. They were now tied to a low branch of a nearby cottonwood. Wearing vests and wrapped in their blankets, the boys were curled up in shallow depressions they had prepared in the sand.

The sound of their deep breathing competed only with the murmuring of the stream next to them.

Running Antelope awakened from his sleep when dawn approached, as was his habit. With eyes still closed, he stretched his arms above him and yawned deeply, then sat up. A solid blow to his forehead knocked him back to the ground. He opened his eyes to see a blur of dark faces as hands grabbed him and roughly turned him over onto his stomach. His arms were jerked behind him, and he felt his wrists being tied together tightly. As he let out a cry of anger, he was pulled to his feet and held up by strong hands as another blow struck him in the face, and then another. Finally, he was thrown back down onto the sand where he lay dazed and bleeding.

21

Running Antelope's head ached, and he could barely see out of his swollen eyes. His nose had stopped bleeding, but it was so full of clotted blood that he had to breathe through his mouth. The Old Enemy behind him had pushed him to go faster at the beginning of their walk. Since then, he had set a faster pace for himself, and was almost on the heels of the man leading them. *That is their chief in front of me. He is the one who stood watching us when the others ran.* He saw that the man was not tall, but looked powerful in his shoulders and arms. He walked in the manner of a tireless traveler like Two Snakes. He was older, though. His black hair, tied at the back of his neck with a thin strip of deerskin, had streaks of gray in it.

When they stopped for a brief rest and a drink from the stream, Running Antelope was able to get a better look at his attackers—and of Blue Stone Shining whose face was almost beyond recognition with dark, puffy eyes and red, swollen lips. The one who had pushed him was about his own age. He had several broken teeth that were clearly revealed when he spoke or sneered. Blue Stone Shining had been walking behind Broken Teeth, with a tall, narrow-shouldered older boy behind him. There were four other men in the group, as well. Two of them pulled the horses along by their ropes while the other two followed at the rear of the column. All of the Old Enemies wore breechcloths and vests of animal skins. Each carried a short, stout bow along with a quiver of arrows tipped with stone points.

Sun Father was almost directly above the group when it reached the camp. This time, cheers accompanied the barking of dogs, and the people rushed over to stare curiously at the horses. They spoke to each other excitedly in a language Running Antelope did not understand. The two captives were pushed and shoved through the crowd to the edge of the camp and told in sign language to sit on the ground in the shade of a large cottonwood. Their wrists were untied, and then tied again in front, allowing them to each accept a gourd of water from a sad-eyed young woman who left immediately without speaking.

Running Antelope leaned over and whispered, "Do you think we can get away from here?"

Blue Stone Shining answered haltingly through his swollen mouth, "They have been...telling us...that we will be...beaten again...if we try to escape."

"You speak their language?"

"I understand...some of their words. They are...like the words...of many who come...to Hawikú." He smiled weakly. "Let us not...try to escape...right now. My mouth...hurts too much...to be hit again."

The boys remained where they were for the rest of the day. No one in particular guarded them, but it seemed to Running Antelope as though all of the Old Enemies, including the women and children, were watching them at one time or another—either them or the horses. They could look across the camp to where the horses were receiving almost continuous attention from the curious. The courageous ones held up fistfuls of grass for the horses to eat. The less courageous were satisfied to lean way out and touch the animals. Those with no courage simply stood back and watched.

As evening approached, the sad-eyed woman returned carrying a basket tray that she placed on the ground between the two. A slight smile tugged at the corners of her mouth when she spoke in Running Antelope's language, "Here is food."

Running Antelope looked up at her in surprise. She appeared to be about the age of his sister. Her long, dark hair was pulled back from her rounded face and bound behind her neck so it hung down her back like a horse's tail. She wore a deerskin garment that fit snugly around her neck and hung below her knees. It was held close to her waist by a tied deerskin belt. "You speak the words of my people?" The young woman smiled shyly and walked away.

"There is deer meat here...that has been dried in the sun!" announced Blue Stone Shining while chewing a small bite. "And roasted cakes...of some kind of cactus...I think."

When Sad-Eyed Woman returned later to bring more water and pick up the basket tray, Running Antelope tried again to talk with her. "Where did you learn to speak words of my people?" he asked in a friendly tone.

"I am from Oldest Village," she replied softly. "I was taken from the fields below the village when I was a young girl."

Running Antelope shook his head in wonderment. "My father told me of such things—and now I am seeing for myself!" Sad-Eyed Woman's face seemed even more downcast as she again turned and walked away.

ᴎ ᴎ ᴎ

Running Antelope slept fitfully that night. His wrists hurt from the tightly wound straps that still bound them, and he was cold. His rabbitskin vest warmed much of his upper body, but without a blanket, his arms, legs, and feet were exposed to the chill. He awakened just before dawn, glad that a new day was arriving. He sat up and looked around at the quiet encampment. Both fires continued to blaze under someone's care, and in their flickering light, he could see the horses standing motionless where they had spent the night tied to a tree.

When white dawn came to the eastern sky, he stood up stiffly and stretched. Seeing no one watching him, he walked across the sandy floor of the wash to the stream that meandered close to the wash's western side. He dropped to his knees beside the water and cupped his hands to splash his face and drink. He then stood and turned around to face the east. Closing his eyes, he thought of his mother and sister, and his sister's husband and baby, and the warmth of their home. He thought of his grandfather and uncle, and the men of the Snake Clan, and the safety of his village. He thought of his mother's patches of corn, and of cotton and squash and melons, and of her corn cakes and piki and rabbit stew.

When he opened his eyes, yellow dawn was rapidly chasing away the darkness. He looked toward the sun's rays as he whispered his greeting, "Oh, Sun Father! I thank Great Power for sending you across the sky. My people can have life because of you. My people can grow corn because of you. Thank you for your light and warmth. I am happy to greet you." He paused to take a deep breath, and then walked back to his resting place where Blue Stone Shining was just waking up.

The camp was coming to life again and the boys watched with interest as they shared a bowl of watery mush that Sad-Eyed Woman had brought them. "These people are preparing to leave!" Blue Stone Shining observed, speaking normally now that swelling around his mouth had gone down. "I guess that means we leave with them!"

"We will see where they intend to go. If they go in the direction of my village, we will not be in a hurry to get away." Nearby, a man had strapped the ends of two long poles on a large, wolf-like dog, one on each side of its husky body. "Look how that man will use his dog to carry things!" The man was now loading baskets and skin-wrapped bundles onto wide strips of deerskin stretched across a cottonwood frame separating the two poles. "The back ends of the poles will drag on the ground! I have never seen that before!"

"I have seen it many times. People who come to Hawikú from the lands of the great buffalo use their dogs that way."

"Perhaps we will soon know how we are to be used," Running Antelope said in a low tone. He nodded toward Sad-Eyed Woman who was coming their way with Broken Teeth and Narrow-Shoulders a few steps behind her.

"We are leaving soon!" the woman announced as she approached the boys. "These two will untie your wrists so you can help us."

When their wrists were free, Running Antelope and Blue Stone Shining followed Sad-Eyed Woman to the center of the encampment where a much older woman stood surrounded by several large baskets, each with a long, deerskin sling attached. The old woman gave the boys a stern look before speaking harshly to them as she pointed to the baskets at her feet. She pulled back a deerskin flap on one to reveal its contents. It was filled with nuts from piñon pine trees like those the boys had seen on the high plateau above the Great Red River.

"She wants each of you to carry one of these baskets," Sad-Eyed Woman explained," and she is telling you not to spill any of the nuts onto the ground." A slight smile briefly softened her face as she added, "Or she will beat you worse than the men did." The boys looked at Old Woman—then at each other—without speaking. Sad-Eyed Woman bent down and picked up one of the slings. "You carry the basket on your back with this across your forehead."

Blue Stone Shining nodded his understanding and took the sling from her. He lifted the load to his shoulder and nudged it onto his back as he slipped the wide center of the sling over his forehead. Bending over slightly to achieve balance, he grunted, "I think I am ready."

Running Antelope lifted the other basket, surprised at its heaviness. He shifted it to his back with a groan and placed the sling across his forehead. He found that bending forward eased the load, and he could reach back with both hands to shift the basket's position whenever he wanted.

Several women and older girls arrived to pick up the remaining baskets, all of which held water. These were shaped more like big jars and were lined with pitch to prevent leaking. The small opening at the top was plugged with a cottonwood stopper. A slow-moving procession soon formed and headed eastward out of the wash. In the lead were the chief and most of the men and older boys, as well as the two horses. Women and children followed, all with loads on their backs. At the rear were men with the pole-dragging dogs and their loads. Running Antelope and Blue Stone Shining were with the women and children.

И И И

At midday, the band of Old Enemies, about fifty in number, entered a large, dry ravine where flat shelves of rock protruded from cliffs offering shade for their rest. Running Antelope bent over to roll the load off of his back and onto the rock-hard ground. After straightening up, he stretched his arms high above his tired shoulders and back before sitting down with Blue Stone Shining to sip water from his gourd.

"Do you know where we are?" his friend asked.

"Yes. Earlier I could see Blue Rock to the south of us. Turtle Shell is to the north. Two Snakes showed them to me not long after we started our journey. They are guides for us, as are the mountains to the west—and Sun Father, too. We are getting closer to my village!"

И И И

The desert nomads stopped in the late afternoon to prepare for the night's camp. A large circle of tumbleweeds and other sizeable plants was formed to serve as a windbreak. Within it, simple shelters were set up using animal skins and poles from the loads the dogs had been dragging. Several men and boys went off to hunt. A trickle of a stream provided the women with a resupply of water. Some stopped to pick ground cherries from leafy vines along its bank. Running Antelope and Blue Stone Shining worked under Old Woman's direction digging two fire pits, ringing them with stones, and gathering firewood. They slept that night in the light of one of the fires.

И И И

When Sun Father cleared the horizon the next morning, the band of wanderers was already in traveling formation. After they had started off, Running Antelope glanced at the sun, and then gave it a second look as a frown formed on his face. "We are now going south as well as east! Look at Sun Father and see for yourself!"

"You are right. What will that mean for us?"

"Look to the north. We can now see the high rocky places where there are villages like mine." Running Antelope pointed to the bluish line of mesas far off in the distance. "Oldest Village is there. My village is only one day's walk to the east of it, not in the direction we are going."

"Perhaps the Old Enemies want to stay far away from your people."

"Then we should leave them as soon as we can—before we get much farther from my village."

И И И

"I know this stream!" Running Antelope said excitedly. The slow-moving procession had made steady progress for most of the day and had finally reached their destination for the night—another tree-filled wash with plenty of water running through it. The boys were looking down into the wash while the chief was selecting a campsite. "This stream passes near Oldest Village north of here! You and I can just follow it! A day's walk! Perhaps even less! The people at Oldest Village will help us!"

The women and children were soon directed into the wash and the tasks of setting up camp began. As Running Antelope and Blue Stone Shining worked, they studied their surroundings, including the steep sides of the wash and the few climbing routes back up to the desert floor. They noted the rough bed of the wash, crowded with rocks and branches carried downstream during floods, and overgrown with bushes and trees growing in its sandy soil. Its shallow stream was about six paces across and glided south in a moderate flow.

When Sad-Eyed Woman brought the boys a bowl of stew for their evening meal, she took it near one of the fire pits and set it on the ground. "You are to eat and sleep here," she instructed them. Then in a quieter tone, she cautioned, "You will be watched."

Running Antelope took a step closer to her and also spoke quietly, "You must know that Oldest Village is not far from here—only one day of walking." He nodded to the north. She looked at him, her eyebrows raised. "Do you ever think about running away and going back to your people?"

She studied Running Antelope's face and then shook her head, a look of determination about her. "I have my child to think of—my daughter. She has only five summers. Her father is here." With that, she started to walk away, then paused long enough to turn and whisper, "If you are going to run away, wait a while. The men will soon attack a village. Leave when they are away."

A look of astonishment was on Running Antelope's face as he stared after her, her words repeating in his mind. He exchanged looks with Blue Stone Shining and the two sat down on the ground with the bowl of stew between them. They ate in silence, each deep in thought. Blue Stone Shining spoke first. "They could walk all the way up this stream and not be seen."

Running Antelope nodded, his face solemn. "They could come out before the earliest light and attack when everyone is waiting for Sun Father."

"Do you think they will attack Oldest Village or your village?"

"Neither one. It will be one of the smaller villages. Oldest Village has many warriors—too many for the Old Enemies—and my village is too far from where they would leave this stream. They will attack a small village not far from this stream!"

"We must be watchful tonight!" Blue Stone Shining said in a hushed tone. "When we see their men leave, we will leave soon after!"

"They will move slowly along the stream," Running Antelope added emphatically. "We will go up to the high ground and run!"

22

Running Antelope and Blue Stone Shining remained awake all night waiting for the raiding party to leave. As yellow dawn filled the eastern sky with its glow, the two looked at each other and shook their heads. "They might stay here for several days!" Running Antelope said with disappointment in his voice. "They could attack in the darkness of tomorrow morning, or the next! We do not know!"

"Look around us, though. I see poles being strapped to dogs and skins being folded into bundles. It may be that we are all leaving this place—now!"

The band of Old Enemies left the wash shortly after Sun Father cleared the horizon, maintaining their southeasterly course across the rough desert terrain. By early afternoon, they were south of a wide, rocky mesa that extended further in their direction than its neighboring mesas. "Villages like mine are up there!" Running Antelope moaned in frustration. "I hope people are looking down on us! I hope they are picking up their bows and clubs!"

И И И

By early evening, Running Antelope had become even more frustrated. They had reached a deep wash with its stream running from northeast to southwest, and their new campsite was directly south of the tall, narrow mesa of his village, less than a day's walk away. "I can almost see the houses of my village!" he stormed. "You can see the high rock they are on!" He pointed as if he was taking aim with a bow and arrow. "Do you see it?"

"I see it!" Blue Stone Shining replied patiently, "I can see it!"

"I am almost home!" Running Antelope cried out angrily, "But I am not home!" He emphasized "not" by throwing a sun-bleached stick of wood to the ground, one that he had just picked up for use as firewood. Then, in a calmer but tense voice, he said, "It is my village they are going to attack!" He moved closer to his friend and lowered his voice, "They will walk up this stream, hidden by its steep sides. When they are close to the high rock of my village, they will sneak like foxes over to its climbing path. As they climb almost to the top, my people will greet them with arrows and rocks coming down on their heads! You and I will be there, and we will send our arrows down on them, too!" Now he felt better. The two finished collecting firewood and carried their loads down into the wash.

$\aleph \aleph \aleph$

For the second night in a row, the boys stayed awake, waiting for the Old Enemies to make their move so that they could make theirs. For the second morning in a row, the camp remained undisturbed until after sunrise when it became active again in the usual manner, including preparations for moving on to some other place.

"She must have been wrong," Running Antelope said dejectedly when Sad-Eyed Woman left after delivering their morning mush. "There is not going to be any attack."

"Do you think she is trying to trick us into staying with the Old Enemies like she wants to do?"

Running Antelope shrugged, but said no more.

$\aleph \aleph \aleph$

Sun Father was midway on his course when the long column of people came to a halt to share food and water. There was no shade, but a gentle wind helped offset the sun's warmth. Running Antelope rolled the basket of pine nuts off his back and sat on the ground next to it. He drank slowly from his gourd and looked around at the dry, rugged land that was dotted with cacti, sagebrush, and yucca. He had been walking with his head down most of the morning, deep in thought, and had not noticed the lone tower of rock coming up on his distant left. Now he saw it. He stared at it, trying to see something familiar about the tall butte rising abruptly toward the cloudless sky. He stood up and stared again. "Huckyatwi!" he cried out in recognition. "We were to the north of you, Brother Badger! Now I am to the south of you, but I can still see you!" Then he called to Blue Stone Shining, "There is the badger! He is our guide to..." He stopped as if he had been struck in the face. He turned away from Brother Badger and stepped closer to where Blue Stone Shining was sitting. "Kawaioukuh!" he said with tears forming in his eyes. "The Old Enemies are going to attack Kawaioukuh!"

$\aleph \aleph \aleph$

The chief led them right up to the rocky base of the huge mesa's western side. He selected a campsite near a spring that sent its water out from under boulders and into a basin that overflowed onto absorbing sand. No firewood was collected. No fire pits were prepared. Sad-Eyed Woman did not speak to the boys when she brought them cactus cakes and strips of dried meat, nor when she later returned to pick up the basket tray.

When Sun Father was beginning to set, the boys were surprised to see the chief approach them, followed by Broken Teeth and Narrow Shoulders, each carrying straps made of strips of deerskin knotted together. The chief stood back to watch as Broken Teeth motioned for the two to turn around and put their hands behind their backs. Running Antelope took a step backward, looking frantically for a place to run. Broken Teeth lunged at him, grabbing him around the neck and pulling him to the ground. "Ai!" Running Antelope yelled, kicking and punching, trying to break the other boy's hold. Stepping over to where the two boys were fighting, the chief raised a clubbed fist over Running Antelope's head and brought it down hard, striking him behind an ear. Too dazed to continue struggling, Running Antelope lay on his stomach while his wrists were tied behind him and his legs bound together at the ankles.

Ν Ν Ν

The raiding party left before the first light of dawn. Running Antelope watched helplessly from where he sat, his back resting against a large rock in the center of the camp. They were heading toward the mesa's rounded southern end, a silent line of plunderers on the attack. In his mind, he could picture them and the route they would take. He saw them going around the tip of the high, rocky place to the other side, staying close to the high walls of its base. He pictured them pausing at the beginning of the path that goes up to the village, then rushing up it as fast and as quietly as they could. *The path is too easy to climb! They will kill anyone who gets in their way and spread out to attack the homes and kivas!* He struggled against the straps that bound him as he had done many times during the night. It only made them feel tighter against his skin. "Growing Reed!" he sobbed aloud. "I am sorry, little brother! I am sorry, Standing Blossom!"

Ν Ν Ν

Running Antelope had fallen asleep where he sat, his chin resting on his chest, his dreams filled with violence and confusion. He awakened with a start at the sound of his name. It was Blue Stone Shining. "They are returning! Wake up!" He sat up straight and stretched to get a better view. There was sunshine all about. Women and children were shouting and cheering as the raiders approached, burdened with armloads of plunder. Some ran out to greet them and help with their loads. Once within the encampment, baskets and sacks were opened and contents held high for all to see. There were ears of corn and sacks of shelled corn and cornmeal, rolls of piki and sacks of beans, cotton blankets and cotton cloth, jars and bowls of pottery, melons and gourds, necklaces and obsidian knives, and much more. The merriment continued until the last sack was opened, then died down only gradually.

All but ignored in the gayety was a young girl who had been at the end of the line of returning raiders. She stood with her head down, cheeks wet with tears, hands tied in front of her. A blue cotton blanket was wrapped about her, tied at the left shoulder, and secured at the waist by an embroidered belt. Her right arm was bare, as were her feet. She wore her long, black hair wound into tight buds, one on each side of her head. Blue Stone Shining saw her first. "They brought someone from the village!" he cried out, straining at the straps that bound him as he tried to get a better look. "A girl!"

Running Antelope held his breath, craning his neck to see. "Standing Blossom!" he said with a gasp. "She is my friend's sister!"

"I remember! You told me about them before you fell asleep last night."

"She is being given to Old Woman and Sad-Eyed Woman!" The boys watched as the women spoke to Standing Blossom and untied her wrists. They gave her water and motioned for her to sit down.

"I am sad that your friend Growing Reed is not with her."

"I am also sad." Running Antelope felt a burning lump growing in his throat at the thought of Growing Reed. He did not want to even guess what might have happened to him. "I will think only good thoughts about you, little brother," he whispered to himself, swallowing hard. "Only good thoughts!"

Ƿ Ƿ Ƿ

By midday, the Old Enemies were again on the move and had picked up a faint trail that kept them heading southeast. The plunder had been distributed to the women and children to carry, as well as the dog-pulled travois and the captives. Running Antelope and Blue Stone Shining each carried in their arms a large sack containing ears of corn. From their place in the column, they could only catch an occasional glimpse of Standing Blossom, who now carried a basket on her back.

"Standing Blossom has not been close enough to see who I am!" Running Antelope called over to Blue Stone Shining. "To her, we are Old

Enemies like the others! I must find a way to get close to her so we can talk!"

"That will happen," Blue Stone Shining answered with confidence.

И И И

Walking all afternoon brought the travelers to a shallow wash with a small stream. Since the wash was deep enough to provide protection from the wind, camp was set up in a line of shelters along the stream's sandy banks. Running Antelope and Blue Stone Shining found themselves assigned to one end of the line, while Standing Blossom was at the other end. When Sad-Eyed Woman brought them their evening meal, Running Antelope had his words ready. "We would like to speak with the girl from Kawaioukuh," he said politely. "Can you help us?"

Sad-Eyed Woman fixed her eyes on Running Antelope's and held them steady, her eyebrows lifting. She then raised and lowered her chin in a slight nod before turning away.

И И И

Sun Father was touching the western horizon when Sad-Eyed Woman returned. "Our chief wants to see you," was all she said, motioning for the boys to come with her. The two looked at each other with puzzled glances, and then followed her up the slight incline to the desert floor. Not far away, a noisy group of men and boys stood around the two horses. They were laughing, and shouting out words to Broken Teeth who sat self-consciously astride the stallion. The horse's rope was held by one of the men.

The group quieted as the three approached, and the chief stepped forward to meet them. He said something to Sad-Eyed Woman and she translated his words to the boys. "He wants you to show them how to make the animals go where you want them to go."

Again the boys exchanged looks. Running Antelope nodded at his friend and said, "Do you want to show them?" Blue Stone Shining shrugged, and then stepped forward and nodded at the chief. The chief grinned and stepped back. Folding his arms, he was ready to watch.

Blue Stone Shining walked over to the stallion and took his time stroking its long neck and allowing it to nuzzle him. His audience nodded and cheered approvingly. He held out his hand for the rope and passed it up to Broken Teeth. "Hold the rope loosely!" he called out for all to hear. Sad-Eyed Woman called out the translation and Broken Teeth complied. "To tell the horse to go forward, lean forward and squeeze your legs against its sides!" Upon hearing the translation, Broken Teeth followed the instructions, laughing nervously as the stallion walked forward scattering the men and boys in its way. Blue Stone Shining walked alongside with the crowd following him. "To stop the horse, lean back and pull on the rope just enough for the horse to feel it!" The increasingly nervous Broken Teeth did as he was told and the stallion stopped. The crowd cheered and laughed, calling out words to Broken Teeth that brought a wide grin to his face.

The chief was grinning, too. He nodded as he looked at Running Antelope and pointed at the mare, then to himself. Running Antelope walked over to his horse and took its rope from the man holding it. He greeted the mare as Blue Stone Shining had greeted the stallion, and then motioned for the chief to stand near him on the left side of the horse. After winding the rope around his left wrist a couple of turns, he reached up with both hands, grabbed the horse's mane, and swung himself onto its back. He looked down at the chief who nodded his understanding. Running Antelope then brought his right leg over the mare's back and slid off to land on the ground beside the chief. The crowd again cheered.

Running Antelope handed the rope to the chief. The chief secured it to his wrist as he moved close to the mare, then reached up to grab the mane. After only a brief hesitation, he swung himself onto the horse's back. He sat there apprehensively while the mare adjusted its footing to the mounting of such a heavy load, and then smiled with satisfaction when the horse stood still.

И И И

When the procession began to form the next morning, Running Antelope and Blue Stone Shining watched excitedly as Sad-Eyed Woman approached them. Standing Blossom was by her side carrying a large basket by its sling. They stopped a few paces from the boys. "These two are also captives," the woman said briskly. "They speak your language. You will walk with them today." She smiled her slight smile and walked away.

It took a few nervous breaths before the sparkle of recognition came to Standing Blossom's eyes. With an expression of astonishment on her face, she raised her hand to her mouth, briefly struggling for air. Tears came to her eyes. "Running Antelope! Is it you I am seeing?"

Too choked to speak, Running Antelope stepped over to her and held out both hands. She took them in hers and cried her tears. They stood that way, neither one wanting to let go, until Blue Stone Shining cleared his throat, and then cleared it again a bit louder.

150

By the time the procession began to move, Running Antelope had regained full use of his voice. Standing Blossom walked between the boys, and the lively conversation among them was non-stop.

"Tell us when you last saw Growing Reed," Running Antelope requested in a quieter tone.

"When they took me from my aunt's house, my brother and my aunt were both lying on the ground, not moving," Standing Blossom replied softly. "There was much blood...and there were other bodies of my people."

Running Antelope shook his head, and then looked over at her. "I am sad for Growing Reed and your aunt...but I am happy that you are safe here with us."

Blue Stone Shining looked over at him and chuckled. "I am happy to hear that we are safe! I will remember that the next time I am hit in the mouth!" They all laughed.

"You are right," admitted Running Antelope, nodding his head, a smile still on his face. "If we do not get away from the Old Enemies soon, Standing Blossom will become like Sad-Eyed Woman, and you and I..."

"I will become like Broken Teeth," laughed Blue Stone Shining," with a mouth filled with cracked stones!" They all laughed again.

"Have you heard where they are taking us?"

"No, but I have thought about that." Running Antelope's tone was serious. "These people have no village of their own. They go wherever they can find food. It may be to the east to the lands of the buffalo, or south to the lands near the villages of Blue Stone Shining's people. Or they could turn to the west and find good hunting along the Little River That Joins The Great Red River."

"I asked the woman with the sad face. She talked about a village where people from many places come to trade things they have for things they want. My father would go to such a village." The boys gave each other startled looks.

"Hawikú!" Running Antelope exclaimed.

"Hawikú!" echoed Blue Stone Shining, a grin spreading across his face. "Now I *am* beginning to feel safe!"

23

With a heavy load on his back and another in his arms, Running Antelope was glad that the pace was now slower and the stops more frequent. He liked being able to refill his gourd from water baskets carried by others, too. "We have slept beside water every night," he remarked to Blue Stone Shining. "We have had enough to drink and so have the horses."

"That has been good, but we have not been able to rest until darkness comes. The chief and his men want to ride on the horses as long as there is light!"

Running Antelope chuckled. "Never in my dreams did I ever see myself showing Old Enemies—or anyone else—how to ride on a giant dog!"

"The chief is always the first to ride! He likes to show the others that he is the best."

"And he always chooses your big horse—and wants to be the last to ride, too, so he can make it run into the camp for all of his people to see!"

"Yes...and he stops the horse so fast that sand and dust fly into the air!"

"He does that every time!" The boys laughed so hard their eyes watered.

H H H

Contact with Standing Blossom had been limited to walking with her in the long column. She spent evenings with the women and older girls preparing food, and nights with Sad-Eyed Woman's family. Running Antelope and Blue Stone Shining spent each night close to a fire pit where they could be easily watched. They found, however, that the more they helped with the horseback riding, the easier it became for them to wander freely within the boundaries of the campsites. By the fourth evening of Standing Blossom's captivity, they were able to visit with her near her sleeping place.

"Will we arrive at your village soon?" Standing Blossom asked Blue

152

Stone Shining. The three were seated together near the shelter of poles and hides Sad-Eyed Woman and her husband had erected for the night.

"The three of us could be there before darkness comes tomorrow if we were by ourselves, but these people are just as slow as the white-faces, so it will be two days, not one."

"Have you heard Sad-Eyed Woman say anything about white-faces?" Running Antelope asked, looking at Standing Blossom.

"No, and I have not talked about them either since...my father and my mother..."

Running Antelope gazed at her thoughtfully. "I am thinking that the Old Enemies know nothing about the white-faces! They may have never seen them!"

Blue Stone Shining turned his head to look at his friend. "You may be right! They have acted as though our horses are the only horses they have ever seen."

"And they show no fear about going to Hawikú where there are many white-faces. I believe they do not know about them!"

И И И

Hawikú was the largest of six A:shiwi villages located on or near the A:shiwi River, a wide stream flowing across arid lands from northeast to southwest, and ending where it meets the Little River That Joins The Great Red River, a two-day walk downstream from the villages. It was home to more than one thousand A:shiwi, and served as a major trading center for people from distant places in all directions. From the northwest came pottery and dyed cotton cloth. From the east came bison hides, pottery, and rocks of schist, and from the southeast stones of turquoise. Brightly feathered parrots and macaws were brought from the south, and shells and coral came from the saltwater sea to the southwest and the Great Sea to the west.

The large force of Spanish soldiers and armed native allies that attacked Hawikú had come from the south along well-established trails used by traders. The expedition, led by Francisco Vásquez de Coronado, had arrived at the A:shiwi River only ten days before Running Antelope left for Kawaioukuh with his father, uncle, Big Bull Snake, and Two Snakes.

The band of Old Enemies arrived at the A:shiwi River in late afternoon and selected a campsite on its north side, a short walk from the water. To the north and east were low, rock-strewn hills that provided protection from strong winds. Across the river to the southeast was Hawikú, the tops of its three-story buildings of adjoining homes visible from the campsite. Also across the river, but too far to the southwest to see, was Coronado's encampment. A well-worn trail upriver, across a small feeder stream, then to the east a short distance, connected the Spaniards with Hawikú.

"I am home again!" Blue Stone Shining cheerfully reminded Running Antelope as they set stones in place for a fire pit.

"Almost! When we get away from here you will be, and I will be closer to reaching my home! We must make that happen soon!"

Blue Stone Shining completed the circle with its final stone and stood up. "The Old Enemies will soon see white-faces for the first time."

"They will see more horses, too!"

"Then they will know where our horses came from!"

"And if the white-faces see our horses, they will want them back!"

"I would like that to happen...but I want to be far out of their way!"

The boys were still talking by the fire pit when Sad-Eyed Women brought them their evening meal. She set the bowl between them and stepped back, but did not abruptly leave like she usually did. Running Antelope looked up at her and smiled. "Thank you for the stew!"

She nodded, then spoke just above a whisper, "You should know that they are almost finished with you." Running Antelope's smile disappeared and a questioning look replaced it. Blue Stone Shining sat up straight and leaned in to listen. "They have kept you with them to learn about the two animals. When they have learned enough, you will be killed."

"Why would they kill us?" Blue Stone Shining snapped, his eyes blazing with anger. "What have we done to them?"

"That is their way. They do not want you to bring warriors from your village to attack them."

Running Antelope's voice shook with emotion when he asked, "What about Standing Blossom, our friend from Kawaioukuh? What will happen to her?"

"She will be useful to them. She can make bowls from clay and baskets from reeds. She will have one of them as husband, and will show her children how to make the same things. She will be...like me." With that said, Sad-Eyed Women lowered her eyes and walked away.

The boys remained seated on the ground, deep in thought, ignoring the bowl of food. Blue Stone Shining broke the silence. "Let us eat. Broken Teeth is coming. He will want to ride my horse."

A wide grin exposed the jagged remains of the boy's front teeth as he approached them. "Horse!" he said, widening his grin even further. He pointed at the two horses being ridden by Narrow Shoulders and another older boy. They were heading toward the river and were followed by a noisy group of younger boys who were chattering and laughing, eager for their first ride.

"Horse!" Broken teeth said again, motioning for the two to come with him.

"Let us see where they are going," Running Antelope said with interest, getting to his feet.

"Yes, let us do that! The river might be a good place to meet white-faces who camp near there!" Both chuckled at the thought. They followed Broken Teeth well beyond the edge of camp to a sandy stretch of land alongside the rushing stream. The others were there with the two horses, waiting expectantly.

"Narrow Shoulders and his friend like to sit on the horses in front of the smaller boys," Blue Stone Shining remarked. "They try to act like big warriors!"

"Perhaps they will show the young ones how to ride."

"I do not think so. Broken Teeth will not let them do that."

When Broken Teeth barked words at the riders in a tone of authority, the two quickly slid off the horses and handed the ropes to Running Antelope and Blue Stone Shining. Broken Teeth then pointed at two of the younger boys and spoke to them in his commanding way. They squealed with delight and rushed over to stand near the horses, one next to Running Antelope, and the other beside Blue Stone Shining. Their smiles flashed white teeth as they looked up at their instructors, eyes shining with anticipation.

Running Antelope began by demonstrating how to mount the horse, and while sitting on the mare's back, looked across the river for signs of life. Seeing none, he slid off and let the boy try the mount and the dismount. He had the boy repeat them several times, and then mounted the horse himself. He glanced across the river again while demonstrating forward movement and stopping, and then slid off to let the boy try. It was when he and Blue Stone Shining began giving the next two boys demonstrations that he finally saw what he had been looking for. "I see some who camp near here out for a ride on their horses!"

"I see them, too! Four of them! I think it would be friendly to wave!"

"Perhaps we should shake our fists instead!" replied Running Antelope, raising his arm to do just that. The four Spaniards did not notice them at first, until Blue Stone Shining let out a screaming yell. "Now they see us! We should now go find Standing Blossom!" They wheeled the horses around and applied knee pressure against their sides until the animals were racing back to camp. Broken Teeth and the others, unsure about what was happening, followed at a run. The chief met them at the edge of camp with a puzzled expression on his face. Running Antelope quickly slid off his horse and handed its rope to him, pointing at the four riders now crossing the river. Blue Stone Shining did the same, and then both boys ran off to locate their friend.

Sensing danger, the chief fixed his eyes on the approaching strangers and began shouting orders. The men of the camp responded by arming themselves with clubs, bows, and quivers of arrows and rushing to join him. The women and children huddled in a tight circle at the center of camp, with many holding clubs.

As the men arranged themselves in a line facing the on-coming Spaniards, the chief received his own bow and quiver from one of the men, and motioned for Broken Teeth to take the two horses farther into camp. He then took a closer look at the strangers who had slowed their horses to a cautious walk. The expression of puzzlement returned to his dark, rugged face. His broad forehead furrowed as he gazed at them through narrowed, questioning eyes. He had never seen men with white skin and hair on their faces. The clothes and head-coverings they wore were odd-looking, as were the seats that held them on the backs of the animals. The purpose of the long poles and the knives they carried was clear enough though, so he ordered his men to bring their bows up in aiming position.

The four cavalrymen stopped their horses and looked at each other, exchanging whispers. Abruptly, they swung their horses around and applied spurs to bellies. With ears laid back and rear hoofs digging into the sandy soil, the animals leaped forward and raced at a gallop toward the river. "They are in a hurry to leave!" observed Running Antelope from where he stood with his friends. "But they will return!" he added confidently, "And then we will be the ones to leave!"

И И И

It took a while for the Old Enemies to calm themselves after the hurried departure of the white-faces. The chief moved about talking to those visibly upset or with questions of concern, but he appeared to be anxious himself and had few answers to share with his people. Running Antelope and Blue Stone Shining were sitting near one of the campfires watching their captors return to normal—and listening for distant sounds of horses and men. They were ready to run to Standing Blossom's sleeping place at the first sign of a white-face attack. "Sun Father has gone in...and no white-faces have come to fight." Disappointment could be heard in Blue Stone Shining's voice.

"Perhaps they will come in the morning instead."

"Or perhaps they will not come at all!"

"If they do not come by early morning, we should leave anyway. By tomorrow night, you and I could be dead!"

"If we leave in Sun Father's light, the Old Enemies will be right behind us with their arrows flying at our backs!"

"Then we must leave before the earliest light—whether the white-faces return or stay away. We can go to the little hills and hide among the rocks." Running Antelope pointed to the east. "What do you think?"

Blue Stone Shining slowly nodded his agreement. "We can walk to Chalowa, another village of my people. We will be safe there. Or, we can cross the river and go straight to my father's trading house in Hawikú."

Running Antelope stood up, satisfied with the plan. "Let us tell Standing Blossom before we sleep. She must be ready to leave when we are."

24

Running Antelope hardly slept. He was alert to every sound—a dog's bark—a child's cry—the slightest stirring of the horses. Sitting up, he would look around the camp and listen some more, hoping to identify a sound that would start him moving furtively toward Standing Blossom's sleeping place. Then, disappointed, he would lie back down and close his eyes until another sound interrupted his slumber. The night was long.

Something within him knew when Sun Father was soon to show his white light—as this sense did every morning when it was time to rise and face the eastern horizon. He reached over and nudged Blue Stone Shining, and then stood up. The camp was quiet, and the fires were reduced to flaming embers. He motioned to his friend to follow as he headed cautiously toward the shelter where Sad-Eyed Woman's family slept. Standing Blossom's sleeping place was next to it. He crept silently to within a few paces of her slumbering form before dropping to his hands and knees. He crawled the rest of the way to where he could reach out and touch her hand. Her eyes opened looking right at him. A finger to his lips reminded her to remain quiet. He beckoned for her to come with him, withdrawing on hands and knees before rising to his feet and following Blue Stone Shining toward the eastern edge of camp. As he turned his head to confirm Standing Blossom's presence behind him, the silence was broken by shouts from Sad-Eyed Woman's husband. He had come out of the shelter and was frantically looking about in the darkness for the girl placed in his charge. When he spotted her, he shouted again and started after her as other men responded to his alarm.

"Hurry!" Running Antelope called out. "Run!" he yelled again, but his voice was drowned out by the thunderous roar of a musket—then another—then others too many to count.

The three were beyond the edge of camp now, running for their lives as the Old Enemies were beginning to run for theirs. Running Antelope grabbed Standing Blossom's hand and the two caught up with Blue Stone Shining as he rounded the first hill. "We will keep going!" he shouted to them. "Do not stop!"

They raced across the rough terrain in the first light of dawn, dodging large rocks and clusters of cacti until they were beyond a second hill. The shouts and screams from the encampment gradually faded away, and they slowed, breathing heavily, needing to catch their breaths. "The last time I heard those sounds was when the white-faces were in my village!" Standing Blossom said, her voice trembling. "It frightens me to hear them again!"

"It frightens me, too!" said Blue Stone Shining, shaking his head. "It was the same when they attacked Hawikú, except we knew they were coming. Our women and children were sent to other villages before the fighting began."

Running Antelope looked back in the direction of the camp, nodding his understanding. "Where should we go now?"

As Sun Father made his appearance, Blue Stone Shining led them farther eastward toward Chalowa. He kept away from the river until the village was clearly in view. "We will cross the river over here," he said when they turned to the south. "There are large rocks we can step on to get to the other side."

Other people were out now using the stepping-stones to cross going to or from Chalowa. After the three had taken their turn, Blue Stone Shining pointed at a well-worn path heading southwest. "We will now go this way to Hawikú and surprise my father."

Sun Father was well clear of the horizon when the three reached the harvested fields on the approach to Hawikú. "I have never seen a village as big as this!" Standing Blossom called out in amazement, gazing at the buildings looming in front of them. "There are so many houses—and they are so tall!"

"I have never seen anything like this, either!" said Running Antelope, his eyes taking in the view.

Hawikú consisted of six large buildings of terraced, adjoining rooms—between thirty and forty each. From front to back, the first row of rooms was a single story; the second row had two stories; and the third row had three stories. Most rooms were for sleeping or food preparation and eating. Rooms deep within the buildings with minimum exposure to light were for food storage. Thick walls were of stones held together by mortar, and roofs were of branches covered with mortar and supported by sturdy logs. The trees used came from mountains far to the south.

The buildings were arranged around an expansive central area that had been cleared and leveled for ceremonies and celebrations. Rooftop terraces served as locations for ovens, drying racks, and workplaces, and for defensive positions in the event of an attack since ground floor rooms had no doors to the outside. One would climb up a ladder to a rooftop terrace, and then down another ladder to enter the room below.

"We will soon be at my father's trading house!" The three had passed by one building and were heading across the central area toward another. Many people were around them now, and Blue Stone Shining frequently waved or nodded to someone he knew.

"I see so many people!" exclaimed Standing Blossom, wide-eyed. "I see more people now than there were in my village before the white-faces came!"

"I did not know your village was like this!" added Running Antelope, just as impressed. "No one ever told me!"

"My father's trading house is there!" Blue Stone Shining said, pointing toward the end of the building they were approaching. When they came closer, he said, "That is where we go up," indicating a tall ladder leaning against the wall of the ground floor room and extending above the edge of the roof.

Running Antelope followed his friends up the ladder. "Oh-ee-e!" he sang out, stepping off the top rung and onto the terrace floor. "There is so much to see here!" The terrace was crowded with trading goods on display. Items were laid out on the floor or hung from wooden racks. "Look at these!" he said, stopping next to piles of abalone and conch shells. "I have never seen shells so big!"

"My father does his trading here and inside," said Blue Stone Shining as they walked across the terrace toward an open doorway to a second-level room. "We eat and sleep in the two rooms below." Upon entering the trading room, he cheered, "My uncle is here!" Two men stood in the center of the room between stacks of woven baskets and a large assortment of grooved stone axes. Both had expressions of surprise on their faces when they saw the three enter. One was Gray Fox Comes Out. "My father!" Blue Stone Shining called to the other man who appeared to be the younger of the two. He was also taller, solidly built, and his shiny black shoulder-length hair had no gray in it. He smiled broadly revealing a full set of white teeth that contrasted with the dark skin of his face. He rushed over to his son and the two gripped arms in a firm embrace.

Blue Stone Shining greeted his uncle the same way, then turned back to his father and said in their language, "My father, I have two friends with me. We have been through many difficulties together. They are Hópitu and want to return to their homes."

Father faced Running Antelope and Standing Blossom and bowed slightly. "Hou! Hou!" he uttered a breath greeting. Then in the language of the Hópitu he said, "I welcome you both. Thank you for your friendship with my son." Looking at Running Antelope, he added, "My brother has told me about you and your journey with the Spaniards. He came back only two days ago with much to say."

Running Antelope returned the bow as he remembered his grandfather doing when he met Gray Fox Comes Out—so long ago, it seemed. "Thank you for welcoming us," he said. "We are happy to be here." Standing Blossom smiled her agreement.

"Some of your people have been here! They left yesterday for the salt lake!"

Gray Fox Comes Out spoke up, "They will return in four or five days. They are getting salt for us as well as for their village. They are good men. We have traded with them over many seasons. You can return to your homes with them!"

Running Antelope's face lit up. "Thank you for telling us this!" Looking at Standing Blossom, he smiled and said softly, "You will soon be home."

"Yes," she replied in a whisper, a tear running down her cheek. "I know."

25

During the days that followed, Standing Blossom prepared the meals for the five of them. This pleased Father and Gray Fox Comes Out, since their wives were no longer living and they usually cooked for themselves. Running Antelope worked alongside Blue Stone Shining in the trading house sorting, arranging, stacking, and hanging recently received items now ready for trade. He watched and listened with interest as Blue Stone Shining, Father, and Gray Fox Comes Out engaged in the actual bartering. Their skills with languages amazed him, as did their bargaining abilities. He understood much of what went on because of everyone's frequent use of sign language. The diversity of people coming to the trading house impressed him, too. They were all men, but with contrasting differences in appearance, clothing, and manner, as well as language.

There were white-faces, too. Only Father or Gray Fox Comes Out would trade with them. They always had little to offer, but wanted much in return. Occasionally, a white-face brought in something unusual like a frayed wool shirt or a threadbare blanket, instead of the usual beads and trinkets. In every case, they seemed satisfied when they left.

א א א

During the morning meal of the day the salt gatherers were expected to return, Gray Fox Comes Out made an unexpected announcement. "I have heard that the white-faces will soon leave!"

"Where are they going?" Blue Stone Shining asked in surprise, his mush-filled fingers pausing in mid-air.

"To lands that will be warm when the cold comes here—lands to the south and east."

"Do you know how soon?" Running Antelope asked, a pleased look on his face.

162

"Tomorrow? The next day? The day after that? Soon! That is all I know!" Everyone laughed.

"That is good for our people and your people!" Father said in Running Antelope's language.

Running Antelope nodded his head and reached over to squeeze Standing Blossom's hand. "That will be good for us all."

For the rest of the morning and into the afternoon, Running Antelope kept an eye out for the salt gatherers hoping they would be from his village. He tried to guess who would come on such a journey. *Will Rain Walk be one of them? Or Snake Moves Sideways? Or my uncle Close In the Antelopes?* He found himself getting increasingly restless. "I will soon be going home!" he loudly affirmed to no one in particular. He was working in the back of the trading house arranging an assortment of pottery items when he heard Blue Stone Shining call him excitedly. He turned to see his friend standing by the terrace doorway beckoning to him. "What is it?" he called back.

"Come look outside!" Blue Stone Shining replied, this time in a strong whisper.

Running Antelope walked over to the doorway smiling, his face shining with eagerness. He stopped next to his friend and looked out on to the bright terrace crowded with trading goods and men who had come to barter. His jaw dropped as he gasped, startled by who he saw. Standing near the ladder examining the thick hair of a bison skin blanket was a tall, slender white-face, his head bowed toward the doorway. He wore no helmet, and the crooked scar that passed over his nose from cheek to forehead stood out boldly in the glare of sunlight. It was Galeras.

Running Antelope stared at the Spaniard, unwilling to hide or run, but not wanting to stay and be seen. Old feelings of anger and fear stirred wildly within him. He longed for a weapon with which he could defend himself—or attack. But he did not move. He just stared.

When the cavalryman looked up, recognition came slowly. His brow furrowed and his eyes glowered—then softened somewhat. He lifted his chin and squinted down his nose at Running Antelope, his cheek twitching into a barely recognizable smile. He casually stepped over to the ladder and onto a rung, and then descended out of view.

Ν Ν Ν

The salt gatherers turned out to be from Oldest Village, seven men and three older boys. Even after leaving three sacks of salt chunks with Father and Gray Fox Comes Out, they still had heavy loads to carry, and welcomed Running Antelope's offer to help. They would leave early in the morning.

И И И

"I know that I will return to Hawikú again," Running Antelope said as he and Blue Stone Shining gripped arms. "We will always be friends!"

Blue Stone shining nodded. "Friends always!" he affirmed. "And one day I will climb the path to your village!"

That was their good-bye.

И И И

The salt-bearing group crossed the river at Chalowa and was soon on the same well-traveled path that Running Antelope had walked coming the other way. He told his new companions about the Old Enemies. They listened with great interest and assured him that they would be watchful.

И И И

On the morning of their fifth day of walking, Running Antelope scanned the horizon to the northwest before hoisting the heavy sack of salt to his back. "I can see the high rock of your village. We will be there before the day ends."

Standing Blossom glanced in the same direction, then turned away and began to weep. "I...do not want...to see my village gain," she sobbed. "I have... no family. Only death...waits for me there."

"My village will welcome you!" Running Antelope said soothingly, taking her hand in his. "My family will become your family!"

Camp that evening was alongside a small stream a short distance from the southern end of the large mesa. Running Antelope recognized the streambed as their place of refuge when the white-face guarding the horses thundered his stick weapon at them. It was from there they had watched the smoke rising from the village, and it was from there they later saw the white-faces ride away on their horses.

As they ate their meal, Running Antelope let his eyes wander up the climbing path to the mesa's top. "There is smoke above the village. Food is being prepared there, too." Standing Blossom nodded, but looked away in silence. "I want to go there!" He stood up. "I want to talk with the people whose fire makes the smoke."

The walk over to the mesa brought memories rushing back to Running Antelope's mind—memories of fearful screaming and yelling, and of frightening thunder each time a stick weapon was used against the people of Kawaioukuh. *The horses were out here—and we were afraid of them, too.* Upon reaching the base of the climbing path, he looked up to its top and along the edge of the mesa. He could not see houses, kivas, or people from this view, but he sensed that he was being watched. *Someone is there looking at me—perhaps many people. But I have not yet seen them.* He frequently glanced ahead during his walk up the path, but saw no one until he was almost to the top. A young man—or maybe it was an older boy—was standing next to the burned out shell of a kiva. His suspicious eyes stared at Running Antelope, and he followed each of his steps with the bow and arrow he held at the ready. *I did not bring a weapon!*

Running Antelope stopped at the end of the path and waved. There was no response. "I am Running Antelope! Hópitu!" he yelled as clearly as he could. He took several more steps, arms extended from his sides, hands showing empty palms. *Is that...Growing Reed?* he said in his thoughts, hardly believing that it could be. "Little brother!" he shouted, picking up his pace. "Is that you?"

The bow and arrow slowly lowered, and Growing Reed took a hesitant step forward. There was a look of sadness about him, and there were dark shadows under his eyes, but a smile of recognition began to form on his face that brightened his appearance. "Big brother?" he shouted back, walking now with confidence. "Big brother!"

Standing Blossom saw them coming before they saw her. She dashed out from the sheltered strip of sand that was to be her sleeping place and raced toward them. Running Antelope stayed back as the two reached each other, hugging and crying. They were both too choked with emotion for words to be spoken.

Words flowed a short time later when the three were sitting close to each other near the warmth of their campfire. "I thought you had been killed!" Standing Blossom said, holding on tightly to her brother's hand. "I saw you lying on the ground with so much blood! You did not move!"

Growing Reed nodded. "I remember hearing shouts and jumping up from my sleeping place. I grabbed my throwing stick and ran outside. There were two of them there with clubs in their hands. I swung my stick at one of them, and then felt a blow to my head." He nodded again. "That is all I remember until after they had gone."

"Were you alone when you opened your eyes?"

"At first I was, and then some of our people came and stopped the bleeding from my head. They told me that you had been taken, and that our aunt was dead."

A puzzled look came over Running Antelope's face. "I did not see anyone but you when I reached your village, little brother. Where are your people?"

"They have all gone."

"Everyone has gone?" Standing Blossom asked in bewilderment.

"Yes, everyone. Some went to other villages after the white-faces left. When the Old Enemies came, there were only this many of us." He displayed his ten fingers three times. "We buried my aunt and seven others. Then everyone else left—except me."

"Why did you stay?" Standing Blossom asked, tears falling down her cheeks.

Growing Reed reached over and brushed a tear away with his fingers. "I wanted to wait for you to return!"

И И И

Sunshine was all about when the salt-bearers passed close to Brother Badger. The deserted village of Kawaioukuh was far behind them, and the mesa of Running Antelope's village was growing taller as they walked. Running Antelope shifted the sack of salt he was carrying from one shoulder to the other. "I want to run the rest of the way," he moaned loudly, "but this sack will not let me!"

"Big brother! If you will carry my sack of salt, I will run for you!"

"Little brother! If your sister will carry your sack *and* my sack, we can both run!"

"No, my brothers!" Standing Blossom joined in. "I have no sack to carry, so I will run for you both!" She picked up her pace and passed them at a jog.

"Come back, little sister! We are only teasing!" Growing Reed pleaded. "Come back!"

"Come back, little sister!" echoed Running Antelope. "We want to walk with you!"

И И И

When the three approached the climbing path, Running Antelope gazed almost straight up to see faces of his people looking down at him. He waved a hand and many hands waved back. "I am home!" he said, feeling a burning sensation in his throat and tears welling in his eyes. Turning to his friends, he smiled broadly, "Little brother, little sister...you are home, too!"

Readers Guide

1. Does a reverent regard for the sun seem unusual? For the Hopi, was it rational? Superstitious? Is reverence for the sun relevant today?

2. Compare modern day preparations for a backpacking hike into a dry uninhabited area with preparations made by Running Antelope and his father for their journey to Kawaioukuh and beyond. What are similarities? Differences?

3. What were the fears felt by Running Antelope and Growing Reed at their first sighting of strangers at the base of Kawaioukuh Mesa. Were they well-founded? Unfounded?

4. What were the prevailing attitudes of the Spanish conquistadors toward the villagers of Kawaioukuh? Look up the word *moqui* in a Spanish/English dictionary. See if its meaning supports your view.

5. When Two Snakes gave his account of the killings at Kawaioukuh, what emotions were triggered within you?

6. What were your reactions to the burial preparations detailed in Chapter 5? How about the family involvement? The burial process?

7. When Running Antelope told his family and neighbors about the surrender at Kawaioukuh and the invitation to the Spaniards to enter the village, why did his listeners react with groans and sighs?

8. Hopi wisdom regarding the power of thought is reflected in the words of characters throughout this story. Cite some of those occasions and discuss them.

9. What clues suggest that Running Antelope was developing strong feelings for Standing Blossom? Were they reciprocated? What do see in their future?

10. Did you catch instances of Hopi humor? Cite examples. Can you relate any of them to your own experiences?

11. The length and activity of the snake dance ceremonial period reflect its

importance to the Hopi people. Could it have meant a matter of life or death to them? Why, or why not?

12. The number four apparently has special significance to the Hopi people. Review the contexts of its use. Do you see commonalities? The metaphysical meaning of four is *Foundation*. It can be in the form of a time of preparation, or the four basic aspects of being: Spiritual, Mental, Emotional, and Physical. Do you see a connection with the Hopi view?

13. Discuss Flute Song Pleasing's leadership style. What do you admire about it? What would you like to see him change?

14. Who were strong influences on Running Antelope? Of those you cite, which one do you think was the stronger influence? Defend your point of view.

15. What is your opinion of Two Snakes? What do you like about him? What don't you like?

16. To whom or to what did the Hopi direct their prayers? What was the dominant theme of their prayers? What else did they pray about?

17. Was Two Snakes' motive for agreeing to guide the Spanish a surprise to you? What was your reaction when it became clear?

18. During his final emotional encounter with Two Snakes, Running Antelope stated reasons for not wanting to follow his friend's plan to kill Galeras. Is there logic to his position? Why, or why not?

19. Compare Running Antelope's impressions of the plateau the travelers reached and its view of the canyon with those of the Spanish leader Cárdenas.

20. In what ways did Running Antelope and Blue Stone Shining demonstrate impressive self-sufficiencies?

21. Some people may raise a moral issue over the taking of the two horses. Was it right or wrong for the boys to do? Argue both sides.

22. Were you surprised by any of the events occurring in the last few chapters? Which ones?

23. Was the ending of the story satisfying to you? Was it a happy ending in your view? Were there any unhappy elements to the ending?

24. What did the ending leave you with emotionally?

CPSIA information can be obtained at www.ICGtesting.com
Printed in the USA
LVOW11s2307250316

480747LV00002B/34/P